Amitabh Bachchan, My Savior

Inspired by True Events

Ronan Doyle

Amitabh Bachchan,

My Savior

Magic Maker Studios
An Imprint Of
Great Expressions Publishing
Scottsdale, AZ 85254

My sincere gratitude to:

Sam Nathan, for sharing his story with me.
Amitabh Bachchan, for saving Mr. Nathan.

*Even darkness can sometimes
show a way.*

Author's Notes

This is a work of fiction inspired by true events. As with any work of fiction, artistic license is used to weave the story together, especially when it is a story that spans decades and illustrates deep cultural and traditional differences.

Table of Contents

Prologue

The years on our calendars become known to us for so many things, set into memory for specific events. This year was no different, this being the one in which Ronan Doyle graduated from New York's Columbia University, and notably, like so many graduates, one in which he had no job to go to. At least, let's say he had no job that would be of interest to him, although there were options, of course, none of them appealing in the slightest. Perhaps he was too selective?

Perhaps he had high aspirations for one so young and fresh out of college?

That is for him to know, and for us to wonder.

But to be truthful, when people asked, "Ronan, what will you do after graduation?" he sometimes would answer, "Oh, you know … this and that," or "I have a few irons in the fire."

It was vague at best. Yet at other times, he would assert, "Oh, didn't you know? I'm a writer."

Being a writer—even an aspiring one—sounded grand, a lot better than "I am unemployed."

What it really meant was that he would never be looked up to by anyone and never have any money to go anywhere or do anything. There was, after all, more than an element of truth in the popular tale that said writers usually lived in attics, and they

1

ate dried noodles and packet soups, or sometimes, nothing at all, just smoking weed and procrastinating themselves slowly to death.

All this was what being a writer was mostly all about, so people often said.

Ronan didn't much care; what did it really matter at the end of the day?

If he was unemployed, he would also be living a downbeat life, and he would also be eating mostly dried noodles and smoking himself into an early grave, wouldn't he?

Being a writer was surely much better; at least, it gave him a modicum of self-esteem.

He hadn't even figured out what it was he wanted to write. Yes, this was a clue that as yet, he only harbored the *aspiration* to become a writer; as yet, he had not set pen to paper even once, at least not with a mind that he would have to sell some of it to earn a daily crust of bread.

But there was nothing wrong with that either. Like a lot of people in their early twenties, he considered he was still searching for his true calling, convincing himself there was nothing amiss with taking his time with it. *Nobody at my age knows what they want to do in life,* he said to himself. *Anyway, there's still time to decide. Lots of time.*

So, he knew that writing was his real love, but what kind of thing to write?

Perhaps magazine articles, opinion pieces, columns, he thought. *Maybe. We'll see. But if there's one thing I never run out of, it's opinions. And if I can make a good living from it … Well, great.*

On the other hand, what about fiction? There are so many untold stories, aren't there?

I just wish I could think of one right now. But he could not.

On this miserably rainy day, Ronan, with his bright blue eyes and windswept mid-brown hair that flopped over one eye, had stepped inside a small tapas bar in search of coffee and shelter, hoping for an escape from the relentless wet and the wind. He set down his satchel and damp camel-colored coat on a hat rack by the doorway. He didn't even know the name of this place, but it was a handy location, a low-profile spot somewhere in mid-town Manhattan.

The tapas bar was mostly empty this evening, turning out to be a sad little place frequented by lost souls just passing through, spending half an hour to get in out of the weather, or to escape something else they happened to need respite from. It was just that kind of a place.

The year was 2009, the year of the financial doldrums, at the height of a bad economy. No, not just a 'bad' economy. Let's be truthful here: a *stinking rotten* economy.

The economic crisis had ravaged its way through commerce and society like the Great Fire of London had started with one burnt bagel—something or other like that, not that they really ate bagels in London—and then gone on to devour the whole city. Here in the United States, the economy's downturn had begun with a crash in the housing market, originally lit by poor lending practices in the mortgage industry, soon spreading like wildfire to the financial markets, then on to the auto industry and finally, the bad news was just swallowing up everything like some avaricious beast, leaving a trail of disaster and decimation in its wake.

In New York, all Broadway shows had been cancelled. Restaurants and bars were mostly empty. Magazines and other publications were going out of business, which was not exactly good news for Ronan. Somehow art and artists seemed to be left to bear the brunt as the financial despair spared no one.

So, these days, nobody was even considering hiring a writer, let alone actually doing it; no company even had it in their long-term plans. Yes, it was a terrible time for any writer about to begin a journey as a professional. But if he couldn't write articles, then there was, just as he had contemplated earlier, always fiction. In the best and the worst of times, people would read books.

Soon, Ronan was searching for a story, sifting through the annals of his mind. He probably could have come up with one using his own creativity, but imagination had never been his strong point.

It would have lacked a soul, a heartbeat, he decided. No, what he needed was a real-life story to form a foundation for his fictional work.

He was kind of lost.

And then he ran into Sam Nathan.

***

By the time Ronan had finished his musings, Sam Nathan was the only other patron at the tapas bar. Just a few feet away, Ronan's eyes were drawn by the man's Columbia University t-shirt.

He was a much older man, probably mid-forties, dressed in jeans, tennis shoes, no socks, and wearing steel rimmed intellectual-style glasses.

The tan indicated that he was possibly of Indian descent. Clean-cut he was, and somehow, he did look like a Columbia graduate too, sitting writing on a legal pad.

A lawyer. Working on some case most likely.

Unusual, Ronan thought.

Most people came into these places to *tap-tap* on their laptops, the days of writing by hand on a legal pad in the past. But what business was it of Ronan's, anyway?

He continued enjoying his tapas along with a large glass of the rather cheap Spanish red house wine. After taking a large gulp, Ronan looked up to catch sight of the man with the legal pad motioning to the pretty dark-haired waitress, just silent hand gestures as if in an old movie.

She came up to him and he talked to her for a moment before she headed to the back wall of the bar and suddenly, the music volume increased, drowning out the quiet ambiance.

It was flamenco music now, Ronan's head bobbing to it, relishing the very melodious sounding, soulful tune. The dark-skinned man sat still, his eyes closed tight, enjoying the music. As soon as the song ended, the waitress turned down the volume. He gave her a thumbs up.

After Ronan had finished eating and drinking, he stood up to go to the cashier.

On his way, he passed right by the man with the legal pad, now noticing many crumpled sheets that had been torn off and strewn across the empty chair next to him. A few had floated to the floor. At the cash register, Ronan was greeted by the same waitress who had turned up the music.

"Excuse me. What is the name of the … tune?" he asked. Was *tune* even the right word?

She smiled and said, "Oh, you obviously have an ear for good music. It's Cameron de Isla singing *Nana Del Caballo Grande.* Have you heard of it? As authentically Spanish flamenco as you can get. Cameron was the best."

"No," he replied. "Well, I mean yes. I have now." *Was the best?* Was the singer now dead? Ronan was observant, which was a prerequisite for being a good writer.

Ronan thanked her with a wide smile, starting toward the doorway to head out. On the way, of course, he had to pass by the legal pad man again. This time, his eyes were drawn to what the man was doing. It was then he noticed an artist's rendition of a face on a white sheet of paper beneath the legal pad on which the man was writing. The drawing was quite striking. Ronan liked to sketch portraits himself and certainly thought he recognized a great piece of drawing when he saw one.

Taken aback by it, he stopped instantly then took a few steps back.

Slowly, he leaned forward to approach the man.

Maybe sensing Ronan's presence, the other man looked up with a kind, inquiring look.

Ronan said, "I'm sorry to bother you. It's just that I couldn't help but stop and admire that drawing. It's so well done. You have a great skill. I can always spot a good drawing …"

The recipient of the compliment smiled broadly, clearly pleased by what he was hearing.

"Oh, I wish I could draw like that," he replied. "It was in fact drawn by a young man from California. No, I do not draw myself, regrettably. What do *you* draw?" He was intuitive, and had surmised Ronan must be an artist himself to have noticed the drawing's finer details.

Now it was Ronan's turn to feel complimented. He felt a faint flush creep across his face.

Pleased to have been recognized as an artist and warmed by the other man's openness, Ronan explained, "Oh, me? I just dabble, that's all. If I had to state a preference, then it has to be portraits. I feel that human faces are so enigmatic."

"Oh really?" the other said, wide eyed. "Portraits are among the most challenging, aren't they?"

Ronan felt his head nodding, though he honestly had little idea of what made a good portrait.

Although he also hadn't come into the bar for a conversation, there was something about this man that made him want to continue talking. After all, he was a writer in search of a story and here was a man who was so far piquing his interest and he could not even say why. Initially, it had been because he was captivated by the man's drawing skills, which he now found didn't exist.

Still, Ronan stood here, right by the side of the table. Hoping he wasn't being a nuisance, Ronan decided to broach the subject of those crumpled sheets of paper. The t-shirt also interested him.

Ronan was not much of a talker, certainly not one for small talk, anyway. But something was compelling him to draw out this conversation with the fellow.

"Anyway! I see you are a Columbia graduate," he ventured next. "Or is it just the Columbia t-shirt you like? And what are these crumpled sheets of paper on this chair?"

Despite these quick-fire questions, which others would undoubtedly have considered prying from a stranger, the other man continued to smile as he picked up all the crumpled papers and placed them atop the table. He motioned to Ronan to sit on the now empty chair next to him.

"Yeah, a Columbia graduate, that's me. A long time ago, I went to Columbia for my master's in business. Don't mind this crumpled heap. It's just that for months, I have been trying to write about a personal experience and I just can't seem to get anywhere with it."

Well, this was serendipitous! First drawing, and now writing!

Ronan took a chance and said, "Well, what do you know? I am a Columbia graduate as well. In fact, I just graduated a couple of weeks ago … in English Language and Creative Writing! So perhaps I can write it for you! What do you think? Or am I being too forward and presumptuous?"

"Well, congratulations! With a degree from Columbia, I am sure someone will want to hire you very soon." The man appeared a little reflective and fell quiet.

"So, what do you think? To the writing idea …" Ronan probed, not letting the subject drop. There was some reason these two had been brought together, and Ronan hoped writing was it.

The stranger answered somewhat hesitantly, "Look, I have to be honest and say I don't know about you writing about my recent experience. That's not to cast aspersions, of course, as I'm sure you are very talented. But how do I put it? For one thing, it is a long and rather complicated story. I have been working on this for quite some time as I said, and still, I have no idea where to begin.

"Every time I set pen to paper, it just feels like the wrong place to start, or I'm explaining things poorly. People who insist they know about these sorts of things usually tell me, 'Start at the beginning.' Well, that sounds rather obvious to me but still doesn't make it any easier, does it? It is frankly quite overwhelming. I simply don't know how people get started on writing stories."

Ronan could see an opportunity presenting itself.

Not just 'an' opportunity but *the* opportunity, the one he had been waiting for. Here was a man with a story to tell and in need of a writer, and here he was, a writer in need of a story.

He thanked the glorious rain for forcing him into this tapas bar. He needed to convince this man that they could help each other, and he needed to find out exactly what this story was all about.

He leaned forward slightly in his chair. "Ok, I understand. It can feel like that, especially when you have an experience that is important to you. It can be hard to transfer those memories onto paper, to do it justice. It needs impartiality. Let me ask you, if I may, who is this drawing of?"

The other man seemed relieved that the conversation had moved away from his writing ability, or lack thereof. He gazed at the drawing again. "Oh! That is Amitabh Bachchan. He is a very popular Indian movie actor. You know, like in Bollywood."

Ronan laughed and said, "Yes, I know Bollywood. I have seen more than a few movies. Is he involved in this story about your personal experience?"

The other man's smile stayed on his lips.

This had been an easier route than a direct question about the experience itself. "Indeed. Indeed, he is. And I think without Amitabh, this story would not have been possible. And if you knew Amitabh, you would have to agree that any story with him in is usually a good one."

Ronan ventured further, relying on his instinct that the story here was an unusual one, and would be a far cry from the ten-a-penny *boy meets girl* narratives.

"Ok, so here's a thought. If you can tell me about your experience, I will be upfront. If I can't see a good story in it, or if I feel it will be too difficult to capture in words, I'll be honest and say so. If indeed the story is long and complicated, as you say, then I would be very interested in writing it. The craft of an author is such that the more complicated stories are the most enjoyable.

"All you have to do is tell me what happened, and I can probably get you a rough draft within a month. I have all the time in the world right now because nobody wants to hire a writer, even a Columbia graduate, and I can devote every waking hour to writing your story. You would be doing me a great favor because I was searching and searching for a new story to develop and write.

"And if I may say so, I have been told by many people that I am a pretty good writer. So, if you would share your experience, I would take it for what it's worth, from one Columbia alum to another. The best part is that you don't have to pay me as long as you let me put my name to the manuscript. Who knows, perhaps it will be the springboard that allows me to join the long list of Columbia alumni who went on to carve out a nice career in writing."

He smiled and waited for a response.

The other man seemed to consider this for a moment, then he took his steel-rimmed glasses off, folded them and placed them on the table. He looked at his watch; it was around seven o'clock in the evening. His eyes twinkled as he reached out his hand, finally saying, "Sam Nathan."

Ronan shook his hand, saying effusively, "Ronan Doyle."

It was well past ten that night by the time Ronan had learned the stranger's whole story. There was sadness in Sam Nathan's eyes, despite the smile he gave to his new acquaintance as he stood up to leave. He left his card with his contact details for Ronan, shook his hand again and left.

That is how Ronan came to know about Sam Nathan and about Amitabh Bachchan.

That night when he walked into his apartment, just outside of the campus of Columbia University, he felt refreshed rather than weary from the day. A fire had been lit in his mind and because of its flickering embers already burning inside of him and growing steadily stronger, he found he couldn't sleep, tossing and turning in the bed.

He gave up on his attempt to sleep, got up and looked up Cameron de Isla's *Nana Del Caballo Grande* on YouTube and clicked on play.

When the song ended, he began to write Mr. Nathan's fascinating story.

It would take him almost forty full days to finish it.

Chapter One:

Wake-Up Call

Sam Nathan,
Los Angeles, 2008.

Many people need an alarm clock to rouse them from slumber every morning, while a good proportion of others do not. Sam Nathan was one of the latter, his internal body clock somehow always managing to wake him a few minutes before any appointed time. In his younger years, he would set the alarm for five o'clock in the morning yet would invariably find that he awoke at 4:55 a.m. sharp, then would lie in bed staring at the clock, waiting for it to ring. Often, he would turn off the alarm function ahead of time to save his poor ears and brain from that dreadful cacophony. He would wonder why do alarms sound so awful and loud. And he answered the question himself that most people need something jarring to wake them up. Otherwise, folks probably would hit the snooze button and go back to sleep.

But still, he would set his clock regardless. As he grew older, however, the alarm became superfluous, his natural programming meant that he knew he would wake ahead of time. Sam had learned to trust himself by now, his habitual waking cycle having never let him down.

That was why he found himself notably irritated to be woken from a deep sleep by a faint ring. Not just any faint ring, you understand, but one that sounded like an alarm.

It was obviously not yet time to be up, otherwise he would have been wide awake thanks to his reliable internal clock. This noise could not possibly be anything to do with getting himself out of bed on time. Sure enough, the sound soon morphed from a long trill into a loud thumping noise.

Already irritated, Sam's blood pressure was on the rise as the hellish affront to his ears continued. His head thumped at having been pulled so rudely from a deep sleep, and right in the middle of the REM cycle, too. He had been dreaming.

That dreadful noise was only getting worse!

He was sleepy and his head hurt, yet he forced himself awake to investigate.

It sounded again, this time grating on his nerves.

Leaving his bed to trace the source of this audible intrusion, Sam stumbled about, first tripping over the bedside table, then the rug, and finally, bumping into the low coffee table.

"Who the hell put that thing there? I don't ever have my table there," he grumbled to himself.

This was deeply disorientating and terribly inconvenient.

Had that wretched cleaner been in and changed things around again? *Who gave her permission? I never put my coffee table right where I'll fall over it if I get up in a hurry,* he thought.

Then it came to him … He was not at home in New York City but found himself in a Los Angeles hotel suite.

Loud knocks replaced the thumping, which in turn had replaced the trill of some sort of alarm.

Or a bell …? Still bleary eyed and fuzzy headed from being woken, it took a while before any recognition of the sound came to Sam. Gradually, it filtered through to his awareness.

Well, that's it. Someone's at the door.

Having failed with the thumps made by their fists, the unwelcome intrusive visitor was now using his or her knuckles to knock. It was most probably a man since not many women would want to make such a racket, disturbing a whole hallway of occupants when it was barely daybreak yet.

That was Sam's thinking, anyway.

Approaching the door, he made a fresh discovery; the supposed 'alarm clock' had only been his new phone's ringtone. The phone was lying right there, juddering on the coffee table in the living room, skittering across the surface with each ring. Someone definitely wanted to get a hold of him; between the phone calls and the *rap-tap* at the door, they were making that perfectly clear.

There has to be a better tone than that, he mused, staring at the phone as he passed by. *When I'm done with whoever's at the door, I'll take a look. Certainly don't want to hear that ringtone every day.*

The room was still swathed in darkness, the only light coming from his insistent phone's screen and a sliver of a crack in the curtains, letting in a shaft of the overzealous street lighting.

He fumbled for the nearest light switch, then squinted through the brightness by the door. The knocking intensified, now punctuated by a stern, feminine voice. So, not a man after all.

"Mr. Nathan, open up. This is Detective Alberts with the LAPD. We need to talk!"

LAPD? Los Angeles Police Department? Am I in some kind of trouble? His nerves, already rattled, jumped and his heart set off beating faster. Without thinking while still in his shorts and a white tank top, he opened up, swinging wide the door.

"Police department? What do you want with me?"

He was truly baffled, and also quite mortified. For one thing, what would the neighbors think of all this? There couldn't be a single soul still asleep in this building now.

But it's my own fault. I should've opened up sooner.

Two neatly dressed detectives were standing there, one male, one female, looking far more awake than he felt. They held out their badges. The woman wore a bright smile, probably the one she was accustomed to making to try and calm situations before they could flare.

It was hard to be angry at someone offering a smile like that.

"Mr. Nathan? Sam Nathan? You weren't answering your phone. Sorry for all the noise we had to make; I guess it *is* early, but we like to catch people when they're in, you know … before they head off to work and whatever," the female said in a somewhat sweeter tone than her yelling.

"Detective Beatrice Alberts, LAPD. Can we ask you a few questions? You're from New York? Just visiting?" The questions were coming thick and fast, giving Sam no time at all to respond.

But on the upside, she didn't seem on the verge of arresting him, and she still smiled.

Detective Alberts was in her forties and even in his current state, Sam acknowledged to himself that she was quite fit. Her partner, a few years older, looked physically strong.

Noticing Sam's gaze had fallen on the well-built detective, Detective Alberts waved an arm in her partner's direction without taking her eyes off Sam. The other officer seemed to be mute.

Has he nothing to say for himself? He lets the female do all the talking, does he? Sam thought.

"This is my partner, Detective Diego Morales."

"What brings you to Los Angeles, Mr. Nathan?" the sturdy male finally said, as if cajoled into opening his mouth because he'd just been introduced.

"It's a business visit," Sam offered politely. "I have a client meeting this afternoon in Marina del Rey at 3 p.m. But I'm also considering relocating here. So, I might check out some places and neighborhoods that could work for me. What's going on? Why are you here?"

"We need to take you to the police station. Can you come with us now?"

"What's this got to do with me? I think you've made a mistake; you must be looking for someone else, I'm sorry." Sam moved to close the door. But Morales was blocking the way.

"I understand how unsettling this is," Alberts empathized. "But you'll be back well before 3 p.m. for your client meeting, right, Morales?" She looked to her colleague.

Morales nodded. "This involves a man named Jay Vishy. Recognize the name? Your number's the only one stored in

16

the contacts list on his phone. You're not in any trouble. It's just a formality."

"JV!" Sam was taken aback at this blast from the past. In that single brief instant, his mind flitted back almost thirty years. "Yes, I know the name. We were classmates and are both IIT Madras graduates. Sorry, that's the Indian Institute of Technology, an elite engineering school in southern India, Chennai, as the city of Madras is now known as. We lost touch after we both came to the United States back in 1985 for further studies. After graduating from IIT, he went on to UCLA. I haven't seen JV—Jay Vishy, that is—since IIT Madras. Why on earth would he have my number? And how? This is a private unlisted number."

Sam's private life was very private. He liked to keep it that way, and he'd never have dreamed that this man, JV, would have found out his private number. And why? For what?

Working in finance, discretion and privacy were prerequisites for Sam. He had made a conscious effort years ago to bury his past and through the passage of time, it was now safely buried. But now it all came back to him, flooding in like it was yesterday, years of suppressed memories from a land and time far away. A land in which he was born and where he had grown up at a time far different from the present. A life he had tried hard to forget but now found oddly easy to recall.

The detectives failed to answer why and how JV would possess his number.

Most likely, they would not know either.

The detectives insisted that he go with them to the police station. Sam knew his rights. This was America, and he had rights.

Somehow, he found himself calmly walking over to his phone and he made a phone call. The detectives didn't stop him. The call was to his office in New York City. New York was three hours ahead of Los Angeles and the office would be open for business, he calculated. He spoke to the legal counsel, Jane Nolan, at his investment firm in New York. Jane was short in her message, direct and quite firm. Sam had very infrequent interactions with Jane. He could recall maybe one specific occasion when he had stopped by her office regarding the legalities of some arbitrage trades his department was handling for a client. He had found her to be blunt, straight to the point and very quick at deciphering the overall picture of the rather complicated deal. Her legal approach had been cautious, strictly compliant to the law and customer centric. He had liked her way of approaching things.

As he finished his call with her, he was told to expect an attorney named Jack Gallagher, an old friend of Jane Nolans's from her college days, to meet him at the Los Angeles police station and was advised not to answer any questions the detectives asked until Gallagher was present.

As he started to get dressed, all those memories of JV came right back in a flash. In his mind he could picture JV as if JV was right there in the room with him. Strange how you think you have forgotten about things, yet somehow when least expected all the details, including the small ones, creep back in your mind.

Chapter Two:

A New Friend

Freshman Year,
IIT Madras, 1981-82.

As Sam started his freshman year, he knew that he was part of a select crowd. IIT was India's breeding ground for top-notch engineers and getting in had felt like winning the lottery.

In 1981 when Sam had taken the entrance exams for IIT, around 200,000 students had vied for a mere two thousand spots. Sam was one of those two thousand. He'd never really imagined that would be a possibility when he'd taken the entrance exams. But such was life's unpredictability.

It was during those earliest days at IIT that Sam first came across JV. On one particular day, Sam had left his dorm room door ajar, a habit of his, more for ventilation than socialization given the stifling late-summer heat. In walked this skinny guy with a unique gait, taking short, quick steps. His eyes darted from side to side and there was an intense nervous energy about him; some would even refer to him as high-strung. Ignoring Sam's puzzled gaze, he headed straight for the bookshelf, flipping through the titles while intermittently whistling, nodding his head.

He behaved quite preposterously, as if this room was his own! *How bizarre,* Sam thought, saying nothing in the moment of surprise and bewilderment. *Who behaves like this in a place not his own?*

Finally, the young man turned around to face Sam and extended his hand.

"Jay Vishy," he proclaimed boldly as if in a job interview. "But call me JV." And just as abruptly as he'd entered, he exited the room, saying, "Quite a collection of books you have there, my man, wouldn't mind borrowing some. I'll drop by soon, another time. See you again!"

Sam soon learned that JV was an insatiable reader but an even more prodigious writer, and as happened with writers, he was indeed a touch eccentric—or even odd, some might say.

It turned out he was selective about sharing his work, although Sam did not ask.

Sam didn't push it, valuing his own privacy and respecting JV's just as much. In time, JV seemed to appreciate Sam's nonintrusive nature, opening up about his passion for the pen, yet still rarely sharing his writings with anyone else. His reading tastes were eclectic too, spanning from translations of Sanskrit, Tamil, Bengali, and Hindi classics to British and American literature.

At times, the two young men's interests overlapped. A tacit understanding passed between them.

Being around JV was eye-opening for Sam.

IIT itself was a melting pot of intellect and personalities, and to any outsider, they seemed like a monolithic group of smart, young Indians. Yet, their diversity wasn't just skin deep with varying shades of tan but extended to their thoughts, background, and fields of interest. It all made Sam realize the pitfalls of judging a book by its cover, a lesson that would become invaluable in his later years. In his current profession, Sam had come across clients with all show and shine, discovering they were deep in debt with negative net worth and a fake front of affluence.

And similarly, he'd learned that many ordinary looking folks had some of the deepest pockets and some of the brightest minds. Contrary to the belief that first impressions were everything, Sam often found them to be misleading, either setting unrealistically high standards or underestimating someone's true potential. He learned to seek the inner of a person.

After those four years at IIT, Sam and JV lost touch, JV heading to the west coast of the United States, while Sam ended up on the east coast. Their friendship, rich in non-academic dialogues that had also served to keep them both mentally agile, ended as abruptly as it began—without goodbyes, devoid of future plans to reconnect. Still, Sam was certain that if they had ever bumped into each other, they would have picked up right where they left off, as if no time had passed.

Despite their obvious intellect, Sam and JV had barely crossed the finish line academically, neither man finding any interest in the rote-based and theoretical education offered by the institution. To them, it was a stifling cage of academic pressure, an environment more focused on mechanical learning than on individualism or creativity.

Neither saw any practical use for the knowledge on offer either, both eager to escape that world and its confines, seeking opportunities less formulaic and more aligned with their interests.

JV didn't do slow. Every part of him moved quickly; his feet, his eyes, even his speech pattern was fast. But his mind was on an even higher level. Amid a sea of bright minds at IIT, his was exceptional, his wit quick, his vocabulary expansive. He had an eloquence that made words flow effortlessly, although his fondness for profanity was equally hard to miss.

Once, he and Sam had been at a dull student skit when someone from the crowd yelled, "Somebody give me a rotten tomato!"

JV instantly retorted, "Use your head!"

It was simple, yet in the moment, to Sam it felt like an incredibly clever and quick-witted retort.

Since neither Sam nor JV had any love for their engineering courses, they often skipped class and by junior and senior years, had ceased attending altogether.

Their grades suffered but somehow, they still managed to graduate. How could they not? The establishment could not possibly have put forth the argument that they didn't know their stuff, or that they were not deserving, not intelligent enough. They just oozed intelligence in other ways.

In India in those days, career choices were often predetermined from an early age. If you excelled in math, you would pursue engineering; if you excelled in biology, you'd pursue medicine.

It was so matter-of-factly assumed and stated as if a foregone conclusion.

By senior year, JV had toned down his profanity but amplified his already extensive vocabulary. Had he grown up in the US, he might have been a bestselling author or a professor in literature, maybe even a Hollywood screenwriter. It wasn't just his use of language but the style and ability to convey meaning that made his writing so utterly incredible.

JV was a huge Amitabh Bachchan fan. Really, really huge, although it wasn't until a bit later into freshman year that Sam discovered just how big a fan he was.

Sam's own first encounter with the Bollywood movie star had been while sneaking an illicit view of his hit film *Sholay* outside an open-air theater. It was 1975, and years before meeting JV at IIT, so he could never have imagined meeting such an avid fan of Amitabh Bachchan back then.

Sam and two of buddies had stood on a truck outside the theater, craning their necks over the wall, trying to catch the faintest strains of the dialogue and music. For the entire three-and-a-half hours no less. On the other side, inside the open-air theater, speakers had been spaced and placed for each individual car. Those inside, either sitting in their cars or on foldable chairs or blankets on the ground near their vehicles could clearly hear the audio, the dialogue, the music, fully immersed in the delights of the movie.

For Sam and his buddies on the truck, the sound was muffled and barely audible, but it was still worth it; after all, how else would they ever get to see or hear Amitabh Bachchan without spending what seemed to be a small fortune? Despite these challenges, the film was unforgettable, much like the cast featuring Amitabh among other memorable actors. The huge screen didn't hurt the view either.

This movie was a classic, probably even today considered one of the best Hindi movies of the seventies. Fans, including JV, knew each line of the dialogue verbatim.

Sam suspected that the current generation of youngsters still watched *Sholay* multiple times and remembered the most iconic lines. Indeed, much of the movie's script was as memorable in India as lines from big Hollywood blockbusters might be for Americans. Who wouldn't remember the classic, "I'm going to make him an offer he can't refuse," or "Go ahead, make my day."

When Sam passed JV's room to get to his own, he would mostly find him engrossed in a book, so wrapped up in the pages that the world could crumble around him and he would hardly notice.

But one day, it was different.

Lying prostrate on his bed with a book, JV glanced up to beckon Sam in as he was walking past JV's open door.

"Do you like poetry, Sam?" he asked, sitting up.

Sam wasn't at all interested in poetry but didn't want to offend, so gave a noncommittal shrug.

Not recognizing his friend's indifference, or perhaps not even caring, JV handed Sam a piece of paper. The handwriting was elegant, a stark contrast to Sam's messy scribbles.

Sam was the quintessential math whiz; as long as his numbers added up, the quality of his handwriting was irrelevant. What did handwriting matter in the grand scheme of things? The numbers were right.

JV's penmanship was a different story because it was clear, beautiful, and seemed to make an authentic effort to convey the nuances of a poem he had translated from Hindi to English.

Fistful of Dreams
(Translated to English by JV)

With a fistful of dreams, and a pocketful of hope,
With a burning desire in my heart to do something, to be something,
My rays may not be as fierce as the sun's but are as persistent as those of a lamp.
Just for how long can you stop me from illuminating away the darkness of my boundaries?
I am not that tree raised on fertile soil, nor was I watered by gushing rivers.
My life sprouted just from barren lands.
I am the words written on stone, just for how long will you try to break me with glass?
I am unerasable; just for how long can you stop me?
There is no oppression in this world which I don't have the strength to bear,
Despite all the loud taunting, I have the strength to stand by the truth.
I am deeper than the ocean; just for how long will you cast pebbles at me?
I will move forward step by step, just for how long can you stop me?
Having fallen a hundred times, now I stand proud and tall
With no desire to ever bow down again.
I have made myself what I am today, with no fear of destruction by you.

When you push me into the heat of challenges, my determination glows like pure gold.
Just for how long can you stop me?
Just for how long can you stop me?

Sam stepped out of JV's room and sat down on the stairs by his doorway to read the poem once again. JV followed, taking a seat on a step below him on the stairs. So much for his indifference; the poem had touched Sam more profoundly than anything from his high-school English classes. It was probably the determination expressed in the poem that was hitting home.

"Good one, eh, what do you think? I translated it myself," JV said.

"Impressive. Your Hindi's got to be decent to pull this off," Sam said, in awe as he considered that the original in Hindi must be something else if the translation moved him so much.

In Delhi, where Sam had lived for years, you couldn't survive without knowing Hindi. But the opposite was true in Madras, where nobody wanted to speak Hindi at all. Regionalism was rife in India, and it was rare for a South Indian like JV to understand Hindi so well as to do justice to the poem's original feel in the translation.

Perhaps what he lacked in Hindi, he made up for in his command of English.

JV chuckled. "I may not be as fluent in Hindi as you, but I think I caught the message well. Still, some purity is always lost in translation. Try to read the original in Hindi and see for yourself."

India was, of course, a polyglot's paradise in which most people juggled at least three languages: their regional mother tongue; Hindi; and English. Many could speak four or five languages.

Crossing the state lines was like visiting a different country.

It was not just the language that would change, but also, the writing would be different, and the script was different too. Sam was proficient and fluent in speaking, reading, and writing Malayalam which was his mother-tongue, Hindi, and English, also understanding spoken Tamil, Punjabi, and Gujrati.

And he was probably even in the minority at IIT as many spoke more languages than him!

This multilingualism had its perks, from enjoying cinema made in various languages to climbing the corporate ladder where your language and communication skills with people from all over the country could take you far. It was akin to in Europe, where multiple languages were the norm and played their significant role in propelling a polyglot far in any corporate setting.

JV and Sam lived in their own artistic bubble amidst a sea of future Silicon Valley engineers and aspiring Indian corporate hotshots. They were anomalies, bonding over books and music, from the nuances of Western bands to classical Indian tunes and Bollywood songs, their conversations also providing a safe haven in an otherwise academically conformist environment.

Those early times at IIT with JV were halcyon days for Sam, and looking back, he couldn't even recall storms or extreme heat bothering them.

He was sure they must have found the perfect tree under which to seek shade, or they'd happened to be safely ensconced in their rooms with a book when the rains had come.

However, life had taken a darker turn midway through their freshman year.

It was a Sunday when Sam and JV had their first encounter with something that everyone would experience at least once every year during their four-year stay.

Sam knew it must have been a Sunday because breakfast had been the coveted *Masala Dosa!* The South Indian crepe-like dish stuffed with spicy potato curry, served with a side of coconut chutney and a generous dose of ghee, it was mouth-watering stuff.

Despite it being a Sunday, Sam would have woken up at his usual early hour, headed down to the mess hall and been one of the early birds trying to catch the first fresh cup of coffee.

On this day, he was walking down the stairs to the ground level, where the mess hall was located, when he heard a scream from the bathroom up on his floor.

He bounded back up the stairs two at a time, hearing that unforgettable bloodcurdling cry; there was no mistaking it for the high jinks of students playing around. There was no time to waste, Sam making it back to the second floor where his room was located in record time. There, he saw JV running out of the common bathroom, screaming loudly with a towel wrapped around him.

JV's black eyes were wide as if they had taken in all the horrors of this world in one fell swoop.

Sam had never seen JV—or anyone—so panic-stricken.

He opened his mouth to ask what had happened to so terrify his friend just as JV shouted, "Nari has hanged himself in the bathroom! Can you get the warden please? Hurry! It is horrible."

The bathroom had six separate shower stalls, and just as poor JV had described, Nari had hanged himself from the shower pipes using a white cotton bedsheet. He was swinging there in the first shower stall with the door wide open and JV had been the first to walk in on the scene.

Sam ran down to the ground floor to get the warden.

Nari had been a junior, majoring in computer science, and the incident underscored the underlying pressures all the students felt but rarely talked about.

Computer science was seen as a coveted field; to be a major in it, you had to have a top 100 rank out of the 200,000 taking the IIT entrance exams. Nari was really brilliant until he arrived at IIT.

Sure, it was easy enough to 'excel' when you were in your own village or small school, but here at IIT, everyone was bright, everyone was brilliant, and for many, it seemed everyone performed better. Here, Nari too had soon discovered he couldn't keep up with his new peers academically and was one of many who would find that getting in was far easier than staying afloat once inside. Whereas in his hometown he was worshipped as one of the top 100 students in the country, here at IIT all his peers in the computer science department were also in the top 100. And he was having a hard time just keeping up.

Sam and JV grappled with the complexity of Nari's death. It had shaken them to their core.

Any suicide would but they had known Nari as a funny, approachable guy, someone who outwardly appeared unbothered by his academic shortcomings. No one could have guessed at the turmoil gradually taking over Nari's mind, or at the way he was planning his demise. The sad part was that no one at IIT knew or cared about his academic performance. He had just internalized what he thought he should be. He was just a cool guy who could have walked into a lucrative job upon graduation. If he could have just managed to last another eighteen months or so.

Sam and JV, especially, could never have seen this coming.

He'd been attracted by Sam and JV's independent streak and had hung out with them sometimes, despite the age difference. Nari hailed from the eastern state of Bengal, evident by his unmistakable Bengali accent when he spoke in English. He had often shared drinks and a few laughs with Sam and JV, along with his great love of football. Now he was gone, just a year-and-a-half shy of graduating.

The question that haunted them both was "Why?" The institute's dean had warned the students about the prevalence of stress and depression during their freshman orientation.

Suicides weren't unheard of here but attributing them solely to academic pressure seemed too simplistic. If that were the case, Sam and JV also wouldn't have lasted a week.

No, Nari's situation must have had far deeper roots, and it highlighted the urgent need for the community to explore real solutions for this recurring issue.

Sitting in JV's room later that day as the shock started to subside, Sam shared his thoughts with his friend. "It's more complicated than it appears. This society instills certain beliefs in us that can make our already challenging situations seem insurmountable. Think about Nari. Just like us, he was probably the star student back home, only to arrive here and realize he was just average, maybe even below average. Our families back home can't grasp this either; they have always seen us as geniuses, putting us high on a pedestal, and they believe we should always be the best."

JV seemed to contemplate this, but only nodded as Sam continued, "We're lucky, you and I, in that we have a solid sense of self, independent of what others think. Nari wasn't that fortunate. He was the boy with the golden ticket for his family, the pride of his town, especially for landing a seat in IIT. That's a massive weight to bear, and as time wore on, the chasm between expectation and reality widened for him. The further he fell behind, the more crushing the pressure became."

As they went about their student life, the two young men somehow managed to deal with the loss of Nari. *Time is a great healer,* as they say. But it was more than just the loss of Nari that had shaken them, it was the realization that they might be next.

What of our own mortality? What if we wake up one day and find we can't cope?

These were thoughts that were too private, too dangerous even to share with each other, and too painful to consider when they infiltrated the mind in the early hours of the morning, in the blackness before dawn came. Daylight would make every bleak thought seem somehow better, but in the small hours between night and day, many things felt burdensome, far too much to bear.

Outwardly, and to a large respect inwardly too, they bore this new weight upon them in their young lives, somehow adapting and moving on. They found ways to cope with it, understanding that there was no right way. What other choice did they have?

Months later, beginning to wrap up their freshman year, Sam was taking a walk when he spotted JV at a tea shop just off campus, lighting a cigarette. He had failed to notice JV's new smoking habit, although he had noticed his late-night drinking. JV looked lost in thought, sporting that distant smile he often wore after watching an Amitabh Bachchan film.

"What's with the smile?" Sam asked, already sure of the answer.

Sure enough, the response came, "Just watched an Amitabh Bachchan movie. The man's a wizard with words, probably a gift from his father. He was a writer, you know. There is something about how Amitabh Bachchan chooses his words … His tone, his voice—captivating!"

"I honestly can't grasp the appeal," Sam replied, taking a seat next to JV and ordering his own cup of tea. "You have to spend hours in line for your ticket at the movie theater, then endure a three-hour movie with an intermission halfway through where you have to wade through a crowd, only to return a few minutes later to finish the second half of the movie …

"It all seems like a long day's spectacle to me."

JV's passion for cinema baffled Sam, but it also served as a reminder of how these little escapes kept them afloat through tough times.

Sam pictured it in his mind.

In an otherwise dark theater lit only by on-screen images, the air thick with the scent of popcorn, JV's eyes would light up like a star-studded sky at the mere mention of Amitabh. The man was more than an actor to him; Amitabh was a demigod celebrated in the excited conversations JV shared with Sam. The math whizz might not have shared JV's passion, but he enjoyed the results all the same as a little of his friend's joy and enthusiasm seeped into his own heart and mind.

JV would completely lose himself in Amitabh's latest cinematic exploits, absorbing each scene as if it were a pilgrimage for his soul. As he rambled on, Sam would sit silently listening, amused yet remaining detached. He often wondered if JV's sharp memory had been trained by watching and then reciting the dialog of an entire scene.

To JV, Amitabh offered an escape to a world woven with dreams.

Yet for Sam, that realm felt out of reach, its call somehow muffled by his practical take on Hindi cinema. But it was JV who was Sam's escape.

So, in a round-about way, Amitabh was his own savior as well. Applying the theory of six degrees of separation from Kevin Bacon, Amitabh had undoubtedly saved innumerable souls.

JV saw Bollywood as an exhilarating canvas of human emotion and drama. To him, the industry's predictability served as a comfort, a reliable friend in a world of chaos.

He reveled in the lengthy bike rides to distant theaters, the time-consuming lines, and the carnival-like atmosphere of a packed hall. It was all part of a much-loved ritual for him.

"Every part of it is a chapter in an unfolding saga, Sam," he would insist, eyes dancing with a sparkling inner light Sam appreciated but could never quite grasp.

He would counter, "You're willing to navigate this circus only because at its center, you find a core worth the struggle. Swap Amitabh with a Clint Eastwood or a Marlon Brando, and I wonder and doubt if your journey would still hold its allure. Perhaps there are a few American youngsters who find in Eastwood or Brando what you find in Amitabh. But I doubt that Hollywood stars command the fan loyalty and blind worship that Amitabh does in India. Amitabh isn't just an actor for you, he's your imaginary friend who makes everything worthwhile."

"You have a point," JV would sigh, his voice tinged with resignation. "Amitabh's presence on the screen is my refuge, my beautiful Saturday morning amongst a sea of mundane days. His artistry lifts me from the ordinary, makes me do the extra, the exceptional. Maybe he's my saving grace in a grind that often feels endless."

A few days after this amiable conversation, Sam and JV received their first-year grades.

Neither had passed with flying colors. While they were disappointed, this news was par for the course in a system designed like a never-ending treadmill.

"Whoever came up with this idea of a weekly deluge of tests across twenty-four credits?" Sam questioned, throwing his hands in the air in exasperation. "It's like they're conducting a ceaseless stress experiment on us, as if we are livestock bound for market. We can never be good enough."

JV agreed, adding his own personal gripe. "What's the point of this rote memory thing anyway? I think I have a strong memory but even I will forget what I learned in a few weeks. After all this circus, most will graduate and go on to careers where they will be trained and taught on the job anyway, with no use for the stuff we learned here and promptly forgot here. It's utter madness!"

Both flunked one course each.

With twenty-four credits each semester, both passed on forty-five out of the forty-eight required during their freshman year, which meant they had to retake the remaining three-credit course in the summer session. For Sam, it would be freshman physics, an embarrassing paradox, considering his self-proclaimed proficiency in math. Most of physics is math and yet he couldn't pass it. The abstract theories in higher physics didn't register in his practical brain.

JV had his Achilles' heel too, lost now in the fog of Sam's memory. Ultimately, they found themselves at a crossroads, contemplating whether to continue to endure the trials of IIT for three more years or to abandon ship. It was a fleeting but somber dialogue, pared down to brass tacks. In the end, they knew that an IIT diploma would take them further than the alternative of leaving empty-handed, also wasting all the time they had invested so far.

Then they would have to bear the shame they would bring upon themselves and their families for opting out after being so lauded for their achievements and supported all the way through. If they gave up at this, the first real hurdle, would that bode well for their professions to come? Would they also opt out if they received a bitter-tasting annual appraisal once employed in a company?

Indeed, how could they hope to acquire such a job without a qualification to show for their time? How would either of them explain that they took the coward's way out and abandoned their study?

No, there was no other viable option but to persevere, to grin and bear it and learn to deal with it, then move on to the next day. Well, at least the first year was in the bag ...

Having weathered the storm of freshman year, they emerged, not unscathed, but more resilient.

It was the first real setback in their young lives. Both of them had found all the prior years at school easy to conquer. This was the first time; they both had encountered an obstacle in a field that they were supposedly gifted. The first time it dawned on them there was a big world out there, where the best of the best students were clearly a cut above what they thought was possible. For Sam, it was eye-opening. JV didn't give it a second thought, for he considered himself the best of the best irrespective of the academic record.

The gauntlet of year one had proved brutal primarily because its roadmap was an enigma, a maze without a guide. Yet, once they cracked its code, the remaining three collegiate years seemed less like a minefield and more akin to a navigable, even mildly enjoyable trail.

In any case, both Sam and JV came from lineages in which failure and giving up were alien concepts, the Brahmin heritage setting for them a lofty standard. Despite their innate intellectual prowess, they were conscious that raw intellect didn't always correlate with academic mastery.

And an even newer concept formed in their minds, which was that academic prowess did not guarantee their success either, especially if they found themselves trapped in unhappy careers.

It was a few days after settling on this gritty resolve to conquer IIT come hell or high water, that JV slid a paper across the breakfast table one Saturday morning in a quiet mess hall.

Sam picked up the paper, studying it.

Penned in JV's signature crisp script was a translated work from Amitabh himself. Though well-versed in English, Amitabh always chose to communicate in his native Hindi, a language he elevated with his inimitable poetic eloquence. Somehow, the entire writing on that paper seemed quite appropriate to their recent discussions about whether or not to endure another three years.

Should I Graduate From University?
by Amitabh Bachchan.

It read:

'I went to school, did well and then went on to university and graduated. However, after graduation, I could not find a job.

'I would spend all day looking for a job, seeking out job placements advertised in the newspapers, talking to people I knew and my family knew, also knocking on doors of many companies and seeing if they were hiring.

'At the end of each day, having spent all day looking for a job, I and a bunch of my classmates who were also unemployed would get together at a coffee shop, a place for us to unload all our frustrations. We had studied hard, gone to school, and then had gone on to university. We had studied hard again and graduated from university. We had done everything right.

'Everything was supposed to have turned out well and yet here we were, all unemployed. We would sit together, discussing how lousy our lives had turned out.

'It was during one of these coffee shop hangouts that one of my friends said, "You know, truth be told, this situation we find ourselves in … It really is not our fault. It is really our parents' fault. Why did they give birth to us? Hence, it is their fault."

'I found some solace in this thinking and that night, went home and after dinner, I spoke to my father. It was the first time and the last time that I had ever approached him and spoken to him directly to his face. I told him, "Why did you and Mom give birth to me? Look at me, all those years of hard work and now, I am unemployed."

'My father kept his cool and maintained his silence. He had his own daily routine and used to get up early in the morning to go for his dawn walks. He would wake me up on his way out. So, on this day, the day after I'd had this great realization that my situation was my parents' fault, he woke me as usual. But on his way out, he handed me a piece of paper.

'After I was more awake, I opened it up, finding it seemed to contain a poem. I looked at it and figured out it was a reply to my question from the prior night. I read it and it said:

'Permission (A Poem)

Faced with the fear of life's daily challenges,
our son asked this question, "Why did you give birth to me?"
And to this I do not have any other answer but to say,
"Why did my parents also give life to me without my permission?
"And why did my father's parents also give birth to my father
without permission?

"And his parents' parents also without permission ... "
Life's daily challenges were there before, and they are here
today, maybe more so.
These challenges are here today, and they will be here
tomorrow, perhaps even more so.
You also bear in mind, that you and your wife also should
get your son's permission before giving birth to him.'

Sam erupted with laughter at JV's uncanny knack for sprinkling Amitabh magic into their lives just when they needed some levity.

That summer turned out to be particularly sweltering, especially in Madras where air conditioning was a luxury that the dorms couldn't afford.

The city library became Sam's refuge, being one of the few places with air conditioning. Books were his companions and he felt at home in the city library for that reason too.

Sam was only taking two courses during the summer, so the season gifted him pockets of freedom to read profusely. These days, despite JV's interesting company, Sam was increasingly finding that he could only take him in small doses. He could be very intense and high-strung, becoming a non-stop flip switch of fire and ice, whereas what Sam needed was space and quiet.

It's possible that JV sensed this as he would sometimes disappear for what seemed like days.

It was around this time that Sam also noticed JV's newfound affinity for alcohol, specifically, a local whiskey brand called Peter Scot. The name was a marketing ruse, a lure for those enamored with the aura of Scotch. Peter Scot was as authentically Indian as any spirit could be, and would not have passed a taste test in any Scottish distillery. One sip, and Sam knew it wasn't for him.

But JV had acquired a taste for this vile liquor, and unlike during his late-night drinking habits when he would take any cheap alcohol on offer, Peter Scot became his all-day companion.

JV was a daring experimenter, a trait Sam first grasped when his friend audaciously skipped mid-terms during freshman year, testing the boundaries of academic norms.

Though his first gamble resulted in a failing grade, by sophomore year, he'd cracked the code of just about passing by the skin of his teeth, utilizing the least amount of effort.

Sam suspected that JV had been experimenting in freshman year to find out how much he had to do to pass a class. He had failed the first time, but that failure taught him to calibrate his efforts.

He made the necessary adjustments, proving able to cruise through the remaining three years with minimal effort. JV's willingness to take risks against such crucial stakes should have tipped Sam off to his future audacities. But back then, at eighteen, Sam's radar for detecting human nuances was still under construction, a far cry from his honed perceptiveness by graduation.

While youthful experimentation was common, JV took it to another level, flirting with stakes wielding tangible consequences. His risk tolerance could make a movie stuntman think twice.

The guy's mind raced like a sports car, via quick bursts of insightful words, a momentary pause to refuel, and then another sprint of eloquent wisdom. And the pacing back and forth, as if he was waiting impatiently for something.

At first, the pacing got under Sam's skin, but over time, he learned to ignore it. As someone easily irritated, he had to learn to program himself to deal with annoyances.

Though JV's intellect was a few rungs higher on the ladder than Sam's, their friendship never suffered an ego imbalance.

Their mutual respect was tacit but absolute, devoid of any condescension.

During study sessions, JV would skim through Sam's notes and then, like a magician revealing his tricks, condense hours of his friend's efforts into a concise twenty-minute tutorial.

As long as Sam had known him, JV had possessed a sort of built-in emotional firewall, a sense of detachment almost elusive. Perhaps he'd always had it, rather than deploying it as a figurative crutch for his IIT years. Sam couldn't quite put his finger on it at first, but he knew something was a little off. As the years rolled by, Sam would come to understand this aspect of JV more fully.

Chapter Three:

Expectations

Sophomore Year,
IIT, Madras, 1982 – 83.

That June and July was like an intellectual summer camp for Sam, hanging out with one of the sharpest minds he'd ever met, during a period when they were both young, moldable, yet confident in their own individuality. Had someone pushed them, perhaps threatened them with an ultimatum, they could have aced their classes for one semester, just one semester to prove that they were capable, but that wasn't their drive. They viewed academia as just one road in a sprawling map of possibilities, a perspective which saved their sanity.

Over time, JV began adopting a more Western mindset, despite his traditional Indian roots. Sam had grown up open-minded and exposed to Western ideas, contrary to the wishes of his family.

It was his English teacher in junior high who had introduced him to and fueled his interest in Western literature. Teachers in elementary and junior high would always have incredible influence, both good and bad. As his outlook on life shifted west, JV also started to evolve, inching toward a more flamboyant persona. This change, along with the hint of recklessness, set off alarm bells for

Sam, foreshadowing a future that would lead him down a path unfathomable back then.

JV was tight-lipped when it came to sharing his opinions around new company. Sam noticed that their Amitabh-centric conversations mostly happened in their exclusive two-person club.

Once, during a long walk to the beer store, Sam finally asked him, "Why keep all your Amitabh insights just for me? Why not share these nuggets with others? You have some terrific material."

JV's answer was revealing. "Because they won't get it, my friend. At least you understand it, even though it may not be your cup of tea. It's not about intelligence; they lack a global perspective. They're self-centered, narrow in their view of life and the world. Our campus is missing that universality, that bigger vision, probably because everyone is so singularly focused.

"There are some rare exceptions, granted, but most are one-dimensional. This is where I envy our American and European counterparts. Universities there have students from all fields of studies. We, on the other hand, are forced to suffer the sole company of would-be engineers."

He kicked at a stone and watched it bump along the road. Sam considered his friend. He had become a different person yet in some ways, was the same. He had this incredible ease with words that Sam envied, and a confidence that came with knowing it would take him far. Some might have called it arrogance, but Sam knew this wasn't the case. JV's recklessness was unenviable, however, and something that Sam worried about more and more as time went on.

Each year, the tragic cycle of student suicides remained unchanged, the only difference being the names, and occasionally the method. So many bright young minds became extinguished under immense external and self-imposed pressures.

For most, this educational journey was seen as the ultimate opportunity, a level playing field to bring the brightest minds to the forefront. Being offered a spot at the institution felt like winning the gold pass, yet once inside, it was suffocating, an endless struggle in which only the very best could sleep easy without concerning themselves with the impending challenges of the days ahead.

Families and social circles added weight to these leaden expectations, with well-meant but ill-advised encouragement and reminders to seize this once-in-a-lifetime opportunity, to not screw it up. With hundreds of thousands of applicants vying for just a couple of thousand spots, the stakes felt astronomical. Yet, when hard work didn't yield the expected outcomes, the students, already burdened by expectation, were left to bear the crushing weight of disappointment. In a way, it was better to be like Sam and JV, ones who chose not to work hard and their results proved it. The ones who couldn't handle life at IIT were those who worked hard yet still found their results wanting.

And what if this prestigious institution was not the dream you thought it would be?

Imagine scoring VIP passes to an exclusive party, only to find out once there that it was never the party you would have gone to if you had only known. It was too late when you were already there, wasn't it? That was very much the case for Sam and JV, yet when it came to a young man's prized education, the stakes were so much higher than in the case of attending any party.

It was the true cliché of square pegs desperately seeking to squeeze themselves into small round holes, navigating a world of too-high expectations, knowing they were soon going to be failing even before they had really begun. They had to find ways to survive, adapt, improvise, and live for the moment. They had to somehow make it through each day, day by day.

At that young age, four years felt like an eternity. The students also felt utterly misplaced, like astronauts mistakenly landing on Mars when aiming for the Moon. It was a daily lesson in fitting in without any chance of belonging, and each day already felt like a marathon for them both.

Chapter Four:

Auspiciousness

Junior Year,
IIT - Madras, 1983 – 84.

To Sam, the start of junior year felt like a rerun of the same show, a young new set of players arriving at IIT as freshmen, a new batch graduating at the same time, each one departing for bigger and hopefully, better lives. Sam and JV had neighboring dorm rooms and were also chugging along on their way to leaving the institution with both a diploma and their sanity intact.

That year, the monsoon was like an overstaying houseguest, pouring down rain for weeks on end. Rainy season also meant wet soccer season, which was akin to running in a chocolate milkshake: muddy, slippery, and a full-on workout. JV would kick off the game in the rain-soaked courtyard, and soon enough, they'd have plenty of others join in for a five-a-side match.

The ball was like a waterlogged loaf of bread, drenched and heavy. Tackling it was risky business, almost like ice skating on a mud rink. Newton's law that a body in motion stayed in motion was the referee here; once you started sliding, good luck stopping!

Passersby were treated to a scene from a slapstick comedy, complete with human cartoons slipping, sliding, and face-planting into mud pies. Each fall made them feel as heavy as a bag of wet sand, and the ball required a Herculean effort just to nudge it a few feet. It was not unusual to see a crowd of onlooking students huddled under trees trying not get wet to witness the free show of comedy.

But for Sam and most of the others who volunteered for this mud bath, it was the best kind of chaos. It was a season of muddy bliss, in which worries melted away like sugar in the rain.

Sam felt as light as a feather in a world that often felt like a ton of bricks on him.

Decades later, Sam would still intentionally walk out during heavy downpours under the very grayest of skies, getting thoroughly soaked and appreciating rainfall as nature's blessing.

Simple sources of happiness and joy were frequently what made life worth living.

Aside from their interest in books, Sam and JV also shared a love of music. Sam was much more exposed to Western music, JV to traditional Indian, yet they managed to educate each other and balance out their preferences. JV wasn't ultra-religious, but he followed certain religious rituals and, being more of a fan of the traditional mantras than Sam was, would kick off his mornings with the centuries old hymn, *Nirvana Shatakam.*

Sam walked into his room one day, curious about the chants JV was reciting.

He was never loud—others could only hear him if they were also in the same room—and, with the exception of Sam, nobody really ventured inside to hear him. So, it was true to say JV didn't wear his religion on his sleeve, but he did seem to follow some family traditions, also effortlessly able to translate the ancient Sanskrit script of the mantras into English.

Sam was not easily impressed but JV's wide range of abilities in reading, writing and translating had an impact even on him. IIT did not seem to be the best place for JV or his wide-ranging talents.

Sam would later understand, with years of exposure to the real world, that there was no place for JV that would be a good fit.

The same was true for Sam too, to a certain extent. As he matured, he came to understand it better, but back then it was just a general feeling of unease, that he failed to fit in anywhere.

Of the six verses of the Nirvana Shatakam that JV had translated, the fourth really stood out to Sam. These verses honored Shiva, the destroyer. But JV had struck through the name Shiva and inserted his own in its place, thus transforming the mantra into a strong self-affirmation.

My Nirvana
by Jay V (A Poem)

I am not the mind, intellect, ego, or the memory,
I am not the ears and tongue; I am not the nose and eyes,
Neither am I the sky nor the earth, not the Fire or the Air.
I am the form of pure consciousness and bliss; I am ~~SHIVA~~
JAY, the auspiciousness itself.

I am not the prana—the breath—or even one of the five vital kinds of air,
Not the seven materials of the body, skin, muscle, fat, flesh, blood, bone, and marrow or the five sheaths, those being food, breath, intellect, psychology, and bliss,

I am not the organ of speech, not the hand, feet and not even the organs of reproduction or the excretion.
I am the form of pure consciousness and bliss; I am ~~SHIVA~~ JAY, the auspiciousness itself.

I have no dislike or liking, not even greed or covetousness,
Neither am I proud nor with feelings of envy,
I am not bound to perform the duties or to acquire wealth and I have no craving to desires or to liberation.
I am the form of pure consciousness and bliss; I am ~~SHIVA~~ JAY, the auspiciousness itself.

I have neither virtue nor vice, I have no pleasure or pain,
I need no mantras—sacred chants—or pilgrimage, not even the Vedas, the spiritual texts or the Yagnas, the rituals,
I am neither the act of enjoyment nor an object to be enjoyed or even the enjoyer.
I am the form of pure consciousness and bliss; I am ~~SHIVA~~ JAY, the auspiciousness itself.

I am not bound to death or such fears, or to the distinction of Caste,
I have neither father nor mother, not even the birth,
I have no relatives or friends, not a guru or a disciple.
I am the form of pure consciousness and bliss; I am ~~SHIVA~~ JAY, the auspiciousness itself.

Thought-free I am, my only form is formless,
I am the vitality of all senses of everyone,

Neither have I attachment to anything, now am I free from everything,
I am all inclusive, the form of pure consciousness and bliss.
I am ~~SHIVA~~ JAY, the auspiciousness itself.

A few days into the monsoon season, there was yet again the annual ritual of another student committing suicide. By the time he was in his junior year, however, the shock had worn off for Sam. It was expected. It was going to happen. Decades later, he would wonder why the institution didn't have a counselor or someone to whom the students could talk. It was a long time ago now, and perhaps mental health and stress issues had been a taboo. He sincerely hoped this had changed.

JV had continued his tendency to disappear for days on end, no one knowing where he was going or what he was up to, least of all Sam. During junior year, one of his unspoken fears was that JV would end up harming himself the way many did when they suffered under pressure.

Sam shared that fear with his friend, only for him to laugh it off. Junior year was also when they were all taking more departmental courses, Sam and JV pursuing all mechanical engineering classes, which Sam rarely ever attended despite signing up. He never saw JV during the day, so assumed he must at least be attending the classes. Perhaps he wasn't but Sam had no way of knowing.

Once, after a disappearance of several days, JV returned but he had lost his room key.

The easiest and fastest solution was to get a replacement made against the payment of a small fee. That was the first time that Sam noticed JV's reluctance to make proper decisions when it came to money. For Sam, the most practical solution was to get the key replaced right away. He even offered to pay for the replacement since he didn't know JV's family's financial situation.

The offer was refused.

"Why pay for something that I already have?" That was JV's response. He somehow failed to see that he did not 'have it' if he had mislaid it; it mattered not that the item may well turn up again, for the fact was that right now, it was absent, and a great inconvenience to be locked out.

So, something in JV's mind decided it would be a good idea to ask Sam if he could sleep on the floor in his room. It would only be for just a couple of days, he said, while he waited for the duplicate key, which was eight hundred miles away with his parents, to be mailed to him.

Sam didn't understand his friend's logic, but JV was quite illogical sometimes.

He ended up sleeping three nights on the floor in Sam's room while waiting for his duplicate key to arrive in the mail. The strange thing was that surely, the cost of mailing would be likely to amount to just as much as the tiny charge for a new key.

Perhaps the point was that the postage cost was met by JV's parents and JV had not needed to reach into his own shallow pockets for the funds. Maybe that was the logic behind it.

Anyway, Sam had a few extra blankets and a pillow to hand, so putting up with JV was not exactly inconvenient, and JV didn't seem bothered by the hard concrete floor.

That genius of an idea backfired. JV's parents, being not so logical themselves either, mailed the key to his room number at the dorm. Of course, you can imagine what happened next.

The mailman would habitually deliver all the mail to each of their rooms.

If he found someone's door wasn't wide open, then he would just slide their mail underneath.

To his credit, JV had actually explained the situation in fine detail to his parents, asking them to address the envelope to Sam's room instead but, alas, they had failed to do it. Consequently, the mailman had slid the envelope containing the spare key right underneath JV's locked door! It was also too difficult to reach it with anything, though JV spent a whole hour fishing under the door with a coat hanger but each time he grabbed the item, it slipped away again like an eel.

Well, JV was furious! Why had his parents gone and done something so blatantly ridiculous and directly against his clear instructions, so painstakingly explained to them twice over? He had spent a good ten minutes on the phone specifically explaining the mailman's system of shoving the mail under closed dorm room doors. And since his key was lost, his door would be closed, and the mail would be shoved under the door if addressed to his room. So, make sure to address it to Sam's room number. But his parents hadn't followed his instructions.

Were they getting so old that early dementia had been setting in without him having noticed it?

Everyone at the dorm thought this situation was hilarious, of course.

His door was locked, he had lost the key and the duplicate that his parents had mailed him was now inside his room—which he could not open without a key. It was pure comedy for the dorm, but it had JV fuming. Sam hadn't seen him that angry before, and hoped never to again.

Sam ended up calling the locksmith to come and open the lock, finally reaching into his own pocket and paying the small fee that JV himself was obviously reluctant to part with. It all left Sam still struggling to fathom why JV often avoided the simplest solution. His decision-making process remained a mystery, and in financial matters, he really was impossible to deal with.

That weekend, JV decided that the two of them should sleep on the beach.

Sam shrugged and tagged along, despite preferring the luxury of his own bed over the alleged 'adventure' of a night under the stars. The spot JV had decided on was about forty minutes away.

They packed their sleeping gear on the back of their bikes and set off late Friday night toward the beach. On the way, Sam had a problem with his brakes. Wobbling all over the place, he struggled to stop his bike at one of the traffic lights, trying his best to bring the bike to a halt by using his feet on the road. It did not go quite to plan, as things often wouldn't; he overshot the red light and ran right into a traffic police officer. Hitting a cop with your bike is never a good idea, and appearing to want to mow one down with it at high speed is an even worse strategy.

Of course, to all appearances, it would look as though he had been reckless, not slowing for the lights and careening into a person on the road with his legs dangling either side of the bicycle.

Needless to say, he was hauled to the nearest police station, just a two-minute walk from the traffic lights. The cop led, and Sam followed, pushing his bike along.

JV tagged along behind, pushing his own bike. He and Sam would look like two naughty boys being hauled into the police station for a good telling off, although in reality, only Sam was in the hot seat. But the way they fell silent as they followed behind the officer made them look guilty.

Tamil was the local regional language and the people of Madras—Chennai—were adamant about everyone speaking it. Sam understood spoken Tamil but couldn't speak the language himself beyond the commonest phrases. Even though he was originally from the nearby neighboring state of Kerala, where Malayalam was the state's language, Tamil remained alien to him. Despite the proximity of his native state, Tamil was not even close to Malayalam. As far as Sam was concerned, it might as well have been a totally foreign language.

Along the walk to the police station, the cop stopped, turned and faced Sam. He seemed to be fuming. Both Sam and JV stopped facing the police officer. The cop shouted at Sam in Tamil, awaiting a response and an explanation of the sorry state of affairs that had come to pass minutes ago on the road. He stared at Sam, and Sam stared back.

The policeman enquired in Tamil, "Tamil teri ma?" *Do you know Tamil?*

Sam had a half mind to make a common joke as a response to that question. Sam glanced and looked at JV. Seeing JV shake his head, Sam thought better of it. But in his mind, he almost said, "Hindi tera bap."

The joke being, while in Tamil, "Tamil teri ma" translates to "*Do you know Tamil*," the exact same Tamil words in Hindi translates to *"Tamil is your mother."* And the common joke is in Hindi you respond by saying, "Hindi tera bap." That translates to, *"Hindi is your father."*

JV knew very well that the cop wouldn't take kindly to Sam talking back in Hindi. And though it was obvious the cop didn't speak Hindi and wouldn't understand that Sam was responding saying, "Hindi is your father," it would have been hard for either of them to control their laughter.

JV had been right and it was best to keep mum and not crack jokes at the most inopportune moment.

"You do not speak Tamil?" the officer realized at last, saying this in Tamil, of course.

All Sam could say was, "Konjum, konjum." Tamil for," *Just a little, just a little."*

And Sam still only stared; that seemed to confirm that the cop's supposition must be correct. Now, the cop became even angrier, waving a fist in the air as if punching a specter.

This was too infuriating that the captive who had almost mowed him down had not even bothered learning Tamil. This had to be a sure sign of a lazy young man.

Sam said to the cop in English, "If you want to speak to me in Tamil, I can understand every word but it's just that I cannot speak it myself. You can speak Tamil if you can understand me speaking in English."

He failed to comprehend that this, even if it worked, would not be useful. What the cop needed was a statement. In Tamil. This frustrating scenario only seemed to provoke the cop even further.

He started in broken English, "Why you hit me with bike?"

"I … my brakes failed," he said in English, speaking slow and loud as if that would help the man understand. But the cop was not deaf. "At least I wasn't driving a car," Sam quipped. "I mean, that would've been a whole lot worse. Or a bus, of course … Not that I have ever driven a bus."

It didn't help matters either; despite the cop not understanding more than a few words of Sam's rambling words, the frivolity of his demeanor came across perfectly well. JV was trying hard to stifle his laughter.

The man replied, his face red, "So, better to hit me?"

His English comprehension was not great either, so it was a stilted conversation at best.

"I don't suppose you happen to speak Hindi?" Sam asked next, and that made the cop *really* mad. It filtered into Sam's mind that the cop would rather speak in English, so he would have to try and explain to him as if talking to a child. "Brakes fail, bike … it no stop," he said.

The cop seemed to understand; at least he was glowering at Sam just a little less. Not much less, but fractionally. "Bike lose control, and *wham!* Bike slam into you!" Sam concluded, trying a weak smile in the hopes it might help. "Please, not my fault. I am very sorry. *Very* sorry."

When he said *wham,* he made the gesture of a fist slamming into his other palm with a loud thump. It was graphic but clear, and the cop was now nodding, squinting too as if greatly displeased to know the full story at last. But he seemed to be simmering now, not quite boiling anymore.

Sam, in a mild tone, added, "We are both IIT students, heading to the beach."

It was probably the wrong thing to have said. The cop spat out, "IIT, eh? You think you special? You so special, yes? No! You not special! You must go back. You not come out to city, ok?"

With that the cop turned around and resumed leading the two of them to the police station.

They soon arrived at the police station, left their bikes outside, and sheepishly followed the cop inside.

Sam's heart sank. It seemed the cop was the only one around, so any hopes of finding someone a little more understanding, or even to communicate with more effectively, were dashed.

Either this station was manned by just a couple of officers, or there was a particular crime spree in the area that had called them all away. The cop led Sam to a room, JV bringing up the rear.

The cop sat, grunted at Sam, and motioned for him to take the remaining chair.

JV stood behind Sam. As the cop busied himself at the desk, it dawned on Sam that JV was fluent in Tamil; it was his mother tongue! *Why didn't he offer to help me out? That's ridiculous.*

Sam turned to him. "You do know you can step in anytime you feel like it, don't you?"

JV smiled back, and with what seemed like fluent and elegant sounding Tamil, he said to the cop, "Please, sir, excuse my friend here. He has had a few very bad days."

Now, he had to think of something quickly, and decided to be a little creative in the retelling of the room key tale; he changed the identity of the subject of the story. Perhaps the cop will show some mercy, JV figured.

"You see, sir, to start with, he stupidly lost his room key and couldn't get into his room. I offered to pay for a locksmith for him, but he refused, saying why would he pay when he had a duplicate with his parents in Bombay? So, he was forced to sleep in my room on the concrete floor for three days, awaiting the duplicate key from Bombay. Three days! It gave him a terrible bad back. He aches all over.

"So, he was eagerly awaiting a decent night's sleep again in his bed when the key showed up. But his parents are like him, not so smart. Let's say they are even worse than him, sir.

"They addressed the envelope and wrote his room number on it. And lo and behold, the mailman straight away slipped the envelope under his door to his room. Stupidity knows no bounds in my friend's family; he really should have briefed his parents better. Or they should have cleaned out their ears and heard his instructions. Now, he had the duplicate key to get into his room, but the key was inside his room with no way to get to it. Can you imagine how mad and upset he was?

"His ears have glowed red all day today. And he is very on edge, as you can see."

At this point, the cop started laughing, his eyes watering. He couldn't stop the laughter, almost doubling over and breaking into a cough, so amused was he. Finally, he stood up, propped himself on the wall with one hand and said, "Oh, my, that is a very bad week indeed. Did anything else happen to him?"

"Oh, nothing much. Only riding a bicycle down a hill and finding that the brakes gave way, and at the traffic lights—which were red, of course—he knocked over a policeman as if playing skittles in the bowling alley. You should have seen it, sir. Oh, I forgot; you were there!"

"Other than that, he had a good week, did he?" the officer asked, still weeping from laughing.

"Yes, he has had a fine week. And I have confidence the rest of his week will go the same way."

The two could not stop chuckling, shaking hands with a boyish fervor as if congratulating one another on having made up and exchanged the world's funniest joke.

Sam had no choice but to nod, join in and fake a laugh and chuckle along with both of them.

The cop could barely control himself as he said, "And may I ask, would this be why you are going to the beach? Because this idiot cannot get into his room?"

JV replied, "Yes, I think if he cools his mind a bit, he will realize that paying the locksmith and getting a new lock is not such a bad idea. Anyway, I will apologize on his behalf. Please excuse him because of his affliction, this being that he is neither smart nor lucky. He suffers from a very bad combination of stupidity and bad luck."

JV was smiling all through the conversation.

A few minutes later, the cop let them both go. He shook JV's hand once again and ignored Sam, who didn't say a word all the way to the beach. JV and Sam headed to the beach in complete silence, neither saying a word. Once they had settled down, JV opened a beer and handed it to Sam, who took a swig before bursting into laughter.

JV joined in.

Later, Sam slept like a baby despite the breezy night.

***

At the start of junior year, almost everyone in Sam and JV's dorm was studying and preparing to take the GRE, a test required by almost all universities in the United States for any application to their graduate programs. It was like the SAT but more advanced, specifically tailored for graduate programs. Taking the GRE would require at least six months of preparation for most, at least that was the norm at IIT where the students were always prepared. The test had two parts, one the verbal section and the other a math section which usually proved to be a breeze for most.

It was the verbal section that challenged many. English not being their native language.

On a whim, JV decided to take the GRE in the fall, a good six months before the rest of the class. It was a few weeks later when Sam learned that he had scored in the top one percentile!

JV was excited that his experiment, as he called it, had succeeded since he wanted to pursue an MBA in the United States. There, the GRE would not be anywhere near sufficient but it would help him a little. For business programs, however, the US universities all required a different test, one called the GMAT. Taking the GRE was just an experiment, a test run if you like.

His true intention, of course, was to ace the GMAT, and taking a shot at the GRE first would help him to gauge his ability. The GMAT would bring a more detailed verbal section than the GRE, but this was never an issue for JV; his immense ability with words and the English language was undeniable, and an English component of any test, however difficult, could never faze him.

In fact, his eyes lit up with delight and anticipation at the mere thought of such a test since coming head-to-head with the most complex English challenges was something he enjoyed.

If the test had been in any of the other languages JV knew, he would easily have handled those as well. So, in due course and not at all surprisingly, JV aced the GMAT.

JV had a new-found confidence now, and he felt nothing would stop him getting into his dream school; he wanted to study his MBA at the University of California, Los Angeles, better known as UCLA. Acing the GMAT with a perfect score meant nobody would pay attention to his grades.

Sam knew JV's essays to accompany his application would also be of a very high caliber. As for recommendations, both had Professor Murthy to rely upon, in the Department of Mechanical Engineering. The good Professor Murthy was in his seventies back then, and a very genial fellow who himself had graduate and postgraduate degrees from the United States.

So affable a fellow was he, that he would more or less give a glowing recommendation to anyone who asked him to attest to their academic prowess. His view was that even the weakest performing student at IIT had incredible potential—if not, then they would never have got in at IIT in the first place—and when push came to shove, that student would shine.

He was not wrong. All his students who went overseas for higher studies always excelled, no matter how weak their grades had been at IIT; it was something that never surprised him because in the professor's eyes, it was obvious. He was extremely knowledgeable about the human character, and aware of the opportunities available to smart kids if the right door opened for them.

And smart kids took advantage of any open doors, so he was in the business of ensuring all the doors possible swung wide for tons of former students, all of whom owed their success to him.

Buoyed by JV's success, Sam followed suit and took his own tests, also sending in three applications that summer. He was also intent on pursuing a master's in business, with an emphasis on finance and economics. Though great with numbers, he had hated engineering, so finance and economics had become his interests by default. First, he applied to a couple of the Ivies and then to Stanford, his thinking being that if he was going to the States, he wanted to be where his peers would be of the highest caliber. Aside from Stanford, he chose to apply to Columbia.

The university was in New York City, the business capital of the world.

The other application was to another Ivy League school, the University of Pennsylvania's Wharton School, also renowned as a top-notch business school.

If bad fortune meant that he wasn't accepted by any of those, his alternative plan involved pursuing a master's degree in economics at any number of great schools in India.

In fact, Sam wasn't completely sold on the idea of going to the States anyway, unlike many of his contemporaries who would not entertain the idea of further studies anywhere else.

Delhi University had an impressive economics program, and he had fond memories of the years he had spent there. Though South Indian by birth, which by nature handicapped Sam in learning to speak proper Hindi, his command of the language was actually very good, almost as good as a local. He would have managed just fine at Delhi University and there were days when this was even his preferred option. So, if fortune smiled and he won a place in the United States, so be it, and he would be happy to take that up. But if he 'only' won a place in India, he would also smile.

Sam and JV were quite private in matters pertaining to their plans after graduation from IIT; although they discussed a few things casually, neither fully revealed all their thoughts to the other.

The two of them were birds of a feather in that respect, somewhat insular and self-contained, valuing each other's privacy and of the mind that they had come into this world alone and would depart it alone too. During the interim years, the brief time they would spend on this planet, nothing especially warranted the need to reveal everything about themselves to anyone else.

Sam had come to understand early on at IIT, partly through knowing JV, that human beings were extremely strange creatures in a myriad of varieties of nature's own imagination.

Just as some of the other students seemed strange to Sam, he assumed he would seem equally strange to many around him. Being seen as strange, an oddball or peculiar was not a crime, and perhaps even accepted as normal. In some cases, students valued more those who were quirky.

Chapter Five:

Letter from Afar

Senior Year,
IIT, Madras, 1984 – 85.

It is funny how memories work, but while Sam could remember a good deal of detail from his earlier years at IIT, the senior year became something of a vague memory. The fall semester in particular was a bit of a blur, punctuated by endless essay writing and applications to US universities by many of his peers. Sam found the whole process rather silly.

He felt that in the quest to attract the most interesting and accomplished students, universities had created this stupid process in which the majority of applicants lied about or at least embellished their so-called accomplishments. Then again, how else could all these applicants differentiate themselves from thousands of others? To those in the admissions unit, one student would surely look just like the next on paper, the only difference being where he hailed from, and his wealth.

Sam had already resigned himself to that fact that this crazy, competitive rush, also known as the rat race, started early in life and just didn't stop, only gathering more and more speed and more and more scrutiny. In the process, humanity, individual personality and creativity, were lost.

As he saw it, the herd got thinned, but the ones moving were still being herded in a certain way by the machinery, most of which trundled on regardless, bound by its own momentum.

The mailman did his usual rounds of the dorm rooms, continuing to shove envelopes under the doors into the students' rooms. That last semester of Sam's senior year would be filled with tons of mail from the United States, all from the universities to which they had all had applied.

In those days, it was impossible to distinguish an acceptance from a rejection by the thickness of the mailed letter; they were all typically just a one-page letter in an envelope, and it was only after opening the mail that the recipient would learn of the university's decision.

It was early February when Sam received a rejection letter first, coming from Penn's Wharton. The same week, he received another rejection from Stanford, and the odd thing was, he found himself surprisingly unbothered and not surprised, figuring that his low grades disqualified him. His top one percentile score on the GMAT did not distinguish him from the other applicants who also had similar scores he assumed.

The following week, an equally slim letter arrived from Columbia. He didn't bother opening it.

What is the point? It will only be the same again. 'Dear Mr. Nathan, We regret to inform you that … but the competition has been extremely fierce … We wish you every success …'

His thoughts turned instead to Delhi University, beginning to halfheartedly muse about life in the capital. His mind was already thinking of the sumptuous, sweet treats he could enjoy at Bengali Market in New Delhi. A day or two after the Columbia letter arrived, one of Sam's dorm mates was in his room to borrow a book. Searching for what he wanted, he noticed Sam's unopened letter on the desk. "I never knew you were telepathic, Sam. Such a hidden talent you have kept all to yourself! How long have you been reading letters without opening them?"

Sam chuckled loudly. "Oh, telepathic I am not. You know as well as I do that when you have received two firm rejections, the third will be exactly the same. In fact, pass it to me. I'll bin it."

His dorm mate raised the letter high, waving it around. "You never know what it may be. You should at least open it. If you won't, then I will. Do you give me permission?"

Feeling that it really wasn't worth the effort of rising from his chair, Sam sighed and said, "All right then. Just for you, I'll put myself through the misery of another rejection. I'll look at it later. You don't need to open it. I promise you, I will look at it today."

His friend selected a book, then walked toward Sam, offering the letter. "You had better do as you've said. I will be checking the garbage to see if that letter is in it." Then he thought about it, adding, "Please. I know what you will do. I see the waste bin already sitting with an open—in fact, gaping—mouth. Please, open it now. Do it for me. Then I can sleep easy tonight."

The student stood rigidly, making clear that he was going nowhere until the deed had been done.

He was still holding the missive out in front of him with a raised eyebrow.

Reluctantly, Sam reached to accept it, then opened it, bracing himself for the rejection, sucking in a deep breath. But his apprehension was soon replaced by disbelief as his eyes went wide. "Dear Mr. Nathan," he began. "I am pleased to inform you that we are able to offer you a place at …"

He need not read any more. His jaw dropped, and his eyes, almost momentarily panic stricken, met those of his friend. "Well, I never expected that."

He later found out that the reputation of IIT Madras had made up for his lack of good grades. Though months later, when he found himself mesmerized by the glorious lights and noise of New York City, he found Columbia to be a great university, the acceptance letter itself had been anticlimactic at the time despite the element of surprise.

As is the case with most things in life, it is the journey that is most interesting and trying, while the destination itself does not usually live up to the mighty anticipation.

Sam didn't even bother informing anyone of this acceptance until days later.

JV strode into his room with his quick steps, his gaze also falling on the letter's branded envelope. "So, which will it be, Sammy? Columbia or Delhi University?"

"Which one do you think, JV?" asked Sam. "I will give you one guess since statistically, giving you two guesses in a two-man race would be quite pointless."

They laughed, and JV said with a hint of amusement, "Columbia. New York City. The Big Apple. I see it in your huge grin."

JV himself had been accepted by his dream school, UCLA, which didn't surprise Sam in the least. They decided to go to the US Consulate together to apply for their US student visas.

Some of their dorm mates had already started the process and, through them, Sam had learned that it was not going to be plain sailing. John Woods was a stickler for details. He was the visa officer at the US Consulate in Madras and his reputation as a hard-nosed interviewer was already established among the IIT students. It had recently become harder to get a student visa to the United States, even for IIT graduates, who were generally considered to be a shoo-in.

Due to all this, Sam and JV stood in line from 5 a.m. at the US Consulate. As they entered the gate and into the building, Sam was stunned by the majesty of the tall, young and fit U.S. Marine manning the gate. *Damn! That guy looks fit and strong! Wouldn't want to mess with him!*

By the time JV was called for his interview, it was already 11:00 am. At this point, they were more concerned with filling their empty bellies than the outcome of their applications. Their knees were sore, as were the soles of their feet, and Sam was rubbing his back like a woman expecting a baby anytime now.

JV came out of his interview crestfallen, cursing John Woods.

"Would you believe it? He has rejected me." His demeanor was crestfallen as he explained, "The consular officer believes that none of us plan to return to India after our studies in the US."

"Well," said Sam, though he was obviously disappointed for JV. "That's true, isn't it?"

"Yes, but we will get jobs. I mean, we *would have got* jobs, and we would have contributed to American society. And we would have made the economy stronger. I wouldn't be on the streets. I would be a productive citizen."

There were so many *woulds,* and every one was futile. So, all this applying and hoping, all the dreaming, studying, preparation and planning had been for nothing!

The thing was, if the students were looking to emigrate to the US, Mr. Woods was not going to make it easy for them because every year, tens of thousands of students came into the US, and hardly any ever wanted to leave at the end of their studies. Of course, he could not decline every visa application purely on that basis, but each student had to demonstrate that the US needed them.

Then it was Sam's turn to face the music. Striding up to the counter, he decided that he was going to channel his inner Amitabh. After all, he had received four years of intense training thanks to JV. As if by osmosis, Sam had felt JV's passion, having been exposed to all things Amitabh. In his mind, he felt tall, strong, and fully committed to playing Amitabh's part in this interview scene. He approached it as if it were an audition for an unmissable acting role.

"Congratulations, Mr. Nathan! Columbia's a New York City gem. Being a New Yorker, I have spent plenty of time on campus at Columbia. It is a fantastic place, a great place for bright minds."

"Thanks, Mr. Woods. I'm excited too."

"Now tell me, how do I know that you will return to India after your studies? What is to stop you from emigrating to the United States?"

Sam took a deep breath. "Well, Mr. Woods. To be quite honest, I don't know what will happen after I finish my studies in the US. You see, just a year ago, I didn't even know that I would be applying for a masters' degree in the US. I was thinking of going to Delhi University to study economics and finance. After four years of engineering, I have discovered that engineering is not my cup of tea, even though I am great with numbers. Columbia may turn out to be a lousy experience and I would have no difficulty in returning to India.

"It may, however, be great and I may end up emigrating to the US. I am not sure that many people know exactly what they want in life, and which route they will pursue in their early twenties. The journey is long with many forks and bends along the way."

"Mr. Nathan, you do realize that I cannot grant your visa if you are openly and honestly stating you might settle in the United States?"

"Yes, Mr. Woods. But I was born and raised here in India. As you may know, our national motto is *Satyameva Jayate,* Truth Alone Triumphs. I do not know if I will return to India or not. Furthermore, I feel like I do not belong in India. I will probably feel the same way about America when I am there, but I will not know for sure until I am there. With your national motto in the United States of *E Pluribus Unum* or 'Out of Many, One,' it is clear that you are open to all peoples.

"Especially because I know America opens its heart to someone like me, an honest person, a sincere person, a hard-working and intelligent person. Whether I end up in India or the United States, I will ensure I am an asset to the country of my choice, just as the country I choose will be an asset to me."

"Mr. Nathan! Well, I must admit, you give an impressive answer. Even a hard-nose like me appreciates honesty. I know

I have put you in a no-win situation; if you are answering me honestly that it is likely you will not return, I will have to reject your visa. If you give me some song and dance about how you will return to India and do some good, I may still reject your visa suspecting an untruth. The perils of having to deal with me, one who can change your life in a split second!"

He seemed to find the predicament amusing.

Is this an American trait? Are they always trying to catch people out, just to bolster their egos?

"As impressive as you are, Mr. Nathan, I must reject your visa, unfortunately. However, your response was the most honest of all the IIT students, so here is a tiny little note I am placing in your papers. If I were you, I would take a moment to read it in private. It might prove quite helpful."

Sam remained calm and thanked John Woods on the way out.

As soon as he was out of the room, Sam read the note, written in surprisingly nice handwriting for a man. It said, 'I suggest you re-apply and place your application through the mail this time. You never know what the outcome could be.'

Sam smiled as he left the building and saw that JV was waiting for him outside with a Coca Cola in his hand. He pulled another Coca Cola bottle from behind his back and handed it to Sam.

"Well? How did it go?"

Sam thirstily grabbed the bottle, took a couple of swigs, then shook his head.

"Rejected," he said.

JV's mood had not lightened much. "I think that guy has a thing against all us Indians. I mean, come on, man. UCLA and Columbia

University, and he rejects both our visa applications? If he rejects ours, whose is he granting? Not very many better schools than these! Would I be right in thinking only MIT and Stanford guys get to go, then? What the hell!"

"I'm going to the post office to fill out a new application and drop it off in the mail. I am not done with this thing, not yet anyway!"

Sam did just that, heading toward the post office with JV following in his wake.

The two of them re-applied the very same day, dropping off their handwritten applications at the post office. What was there to lose?

A few days later, JV stumbled into Sam's room, clearly drunk. Even though all their conversations were always in English, he decided to speak in his version of Hindi, laden with bad pronunciation and a thick South Indian accent.

Pretty comical, and JV was totally intoxicated to boot.

"Hey brother, how are you? Enjoying your evening, are you?"

"Yes, Amitabh. Thank you. And how are you?" Sam replied.

He was somewhat lucid, the only thing revealing him as drunk being his attempt to act like an inebriated Amitabh Bachchan.

A half-length mirror lined the inside of the door in Sam's room.

JV closed the door, stood upright, and stared at his reflection there. Then, he began to talk to it in the best Hindi that he had ever spoken. Later, Sam found out that he had been enacting a scene from a 1977 movie called *Amar, Akbar, Anthony,* a scene in which a drunk Amitabh was beaten up by a bully, after which he returned home to address himself in the mirror.

JV went on to talk to himself in what was his version of Amitabh Bachchan in that same movie.

He had gazed around Sam's room, looking very comfortable.

Then he pulled out Sam's black shoe polish, and with the utmost seriousness, applied it around one eye, again mimicking Amitabh in the re-enacted scene.

In the movie, Amitabh was playing a character named Anthony, sporting a black eye from the beating he had taken. It seemed that JV was well into the role, leaning against the wall and staring at himself in the mirror. His reflection looked back with its shoe polish black eye, and JV put on a pained expression, talking to his reflection in the mirror. The drunken slur in his voice and the truly horrendous Hindi with his South Indian accent made the scene hilarious.

Buss, ho gaya pitayi?! Khush? Khush?

[Is that enough now that you have been beaten up? Happy? Happy?]

Tere ko main iska vasteyich bolta tha ki daru mat pi, mat pi, mat pi daru, daru kharab chiz hai.

[This is the reason I used to tell you over and over again, don't drink alcohol, don't drink, don't drink alcohol. Alcohol is a bad thing.]

Tu agar daru nahin piyela hota, to kya woh jadya tere ko marne ko sakta?

Are tu khud Bol, kya tere ko marane ko sakta?

[If you had not been drunk, would that loser have been able to beat you up? Tell me yourself, would he have been able to beat you up?]

Arey Anthony bhai, tum akela das, das aadmi ko marane ko sakata.

[Anthony, my brother, you could have singlehandedly beaten ten, ten men.]

Par tu apunka suntayich kidhar hai! Kidharyich sunta hai?

[But when do you ever listen to me? When do you listen to me?]

He pointed to his reflection with his forefinger, made a sad face and continued.

Dekh, dekh thopda dekh. Dekh thopda aayine main jake dekh, kitna mara tereko.

[See? See, take a look at your face. Take a look at your face in the mirror. How badly you have been beaten up.]

Pakka idiot dikhta hai!

[You look like an absolute idiot!]

He then straightened up and put his hands up flat as if staying 'stop,' and continued talking to his reflection.

Chal tu...tu khada rehne ka hai, hilne ka nhi thoda davai lagaega hum

[Come on now, you need to stand still, do not move. I will apply a medical treatment.]

Then he pretended to take a bottle of tincture and pour it on an imaginary cotton swab as he leaned against the wall to support his drunken self.

He continued his conversation with his reflected self.

Excuse me ... aye hilta kahe ho bhai. Khada rehne ka hai ... steady ... hmm ... steady.

[Excuse me ... Hey, why are you moving? You need to stand still. Steady ... hmm ... steady.]

Dekh bhai abhi thoda jalega ... haan lekin chillane ka nhi kya ... apun log gusse me hai bahut zyada kya ... chillane ka nahi.

[Look, brother, it will burn a little, yaa ... but don't scream, ok? We are very angry right now … So, don't scream.]

He started to blow on the mirror as if to help the tincture evaporate and help extinguish the burning sensation by cooling it.

Steady ... hmm. Jalta hai na ...? Voto jalegaich isiliye tere ko bola hai daru nahi pine ka hai ... daru bahut kharab chiz hai.

[Steady. Hmm. Is it burning? For sure, it will burn; that is why I told you not to drink alcohol. Alcohol is a bad thing.]

Bandage laga deta hoon.

[I'll now apply a bandage.]

He pretended to peel off the adhesive of a bandage, then he proceeded to apply the bandage onto the mirror, pushing his fingers harder against it as if to aid the imaginary bandage to stick. He enacted the entire scene including the hilarious parts in which he applied liniment and bandages to his own reflection in the mirror. Sam found out later that in the movie Amitabh had applied the bandage and the medicine to the mirror, thinking in his drunken state that he was applying to himself, reflected in the mirror.

Kal subhe tak sab sahi ho jaega ... thik hai fikar nahi karne ka. Okay?

[Tomorrow morning, everything will become right. All right, not to worry, okay?]

Accha bhai abhi apun sone ko jata hai. Tum bhi jao ... hum bhi jata hai ... Goodnight.

[All right brother, now I will go to sleep. You go, and I will also go. Goodnight!]

75

He turned around, faced Sam, and took a bow. Then he opened the door and walked out.

Shutting the door behind him, he started singing one of his favorite Amitabh songs, *Mere angane mein tumhara kya kaam hai,* which translates as, 'What are you up to in my backyard?'

It was a popular song from the 1981 movie *Lawaris*.

Sam had smiled through the whole performance in front of the mirror, but the singing, the singing was something else. Sam guffawed like he never had before. It was just way too funny.

At the time, Sam hadn't been familiar with the scene JV had acted out as it was a movie he hadn't seen. But he had seen enough of Amitabh to recognize the speech patterns and mannerisms that JV was using. Obviously, JV was over-acting considerably but that was all part of the charm. His laughter lasted several minutes after JV headed out the door with that song in his heart.

Two weeks later, their passports came back in the mail. Their visa applications had been accepted, and at last, their student visas had been granted. Both were overjoyed and excited upon finding out that their lives were about to change dramatically. They immediately biked all the way to the store off campus to get some cold beers.

Without refrigerators in the dorms, cold beer required this journey of a few miles and this was an occasion that definitely called for it. The beer came in really tall 25-oz or 750ml bottles, not the smaller 12 oz—355ml—ones commonly sold in the United States.

To this day, Sam could not recall how many bottles they had downed that night, nor did he remember riding back to campus. He knew only that it was the last time he ever saw JV.

Then, after the final exams that senior year, Sam went home to his parents in the neighboring state of Kerala. An overnight train journey from IIT, to spend the last few weeks with his parents, also aware of a strong sense of apprehension and a distinct feeling that it would be the last time he would see them for quite a while. They were very traditional and not given to traveling, while for his own part, he had been given the key to the land of milk and honey and doubted he would return to India. What would bring him back here? America had everything.

Graduation was to take place a month after the finals.

While Sam's mom asked her son to attend, his dad said nothing at all on the matter.

Sam suspected that he knew what his son was doing, wanting to spend every minute possible with them. The day Sam left India, his father came to the airport to see him off.

His mom was not happy around goodbyes, so she stayed home, no doubt weeping a little.

As Sam headed to board the plane, his dad gave him a firm handshake, a heartfelt hug, and smiled a beaming smile, though it was also tinged with a certain sadness. He said, "I am very proud of you, my son. I am so happy for you that you are leaving this mess of a country. You are a brahmin from South India, from a lower middle-class family. There are no breaks, no opportunities for people like us here, but you … You have created a break for yourself, a good future, son.

"The United States is home for people like you, a place where intelligence, hard work and perseverance are appreciated and rewarded, irrespective of your background. Deep in my heart, I feel only as if you are going home. And I know that will not make sense to you, but—"

Sam interrupted, saying as he held back copious unspent tears, "Dad, it makes sense. Of course, it does. Because every word you have ever spoken to me has made sense in my mind, and it is because of you and Mom that I have been able to make my way."

They hugged close, Sam still acting stubborn in refusing to let his tears fall.

"Thank you for everything, Dad. I will call you as soon as I get there safely."

Sam never returned to India and his parents never did visit the United States either. Sam called them once a week for a very long time, long enough that they eventually passed away.

But the fact that he knew they lived on in him … that kept his chin up and his heart determined.

Chapter Six:

An Unspeakable Act

Los Angeles, California,
October 2008.

Sam followed the LAPD detectives out of his hotel suite. As they left the building under the watchful eye of the night porter, Sam's initial panic began subsiding.

He wasn't in handcuffs and hadn't been read his Miranda rights, so the chances were that he was not in any serious trouble. At least, he liked to believe so. Moreover, knowing that Jack Gallagher will be present when the detectives question him to protect his rights and that Gallagher came with a glowing recommendation from his firm's legal counsel put his mind at ease.

Detective Alberts simply seemed to think he could help with something, although what that 'something' might be, Sam couldn't even begin to imagine.

He hadn't seen JV since the day they had celebrated the arrival of their student visas, and even that was foggy in his memory thanks to the combined effects of time and numerous cold beers.

How his former IIT friend had gotten hold of his current cell phone number was another mystery. The phone number was not a listed number. So, how did JV get the number for him? But he decided there was little point in wondering about it and making his head hurt.

Sam positioned himself in the back of the sedan where the detectives had motioned him to get in, the two detectives sitting up front with Alberts driving. She glanced in the rearview mirror and made eye contact with Sam briefly.

Then she commenced addressing her fellow detective.

"Morales, what do you think? The 405 at this time of day's best, eh? It's still early."

Morales nodded in agreement, and they pulled away. Southern California rush hour traffic is a nightmare. All the freeways are stop-and-go traffic for miles and for hours on end.

Nobody spoke for a while. Sam now noticed that Alberts had headed north on the 405 freeway exactly as discussed, and from his side window, he could see the faintest hint of dawn on the horizon.

As the detectives were not divulging any further information, Sam took the bull by the horns.

"I was wondering which LAPD department you're from," he inquired, leaning forward.

It was Morales who answered. "Homicide."

Sam's stomach jumped, and his mind raced.

Homicide! What the heck did JV get himself involved in? Well, something to do with killing people, obviously. But there was nothing to indicate he was accused of being a perpetrator. He could have become tangled in this in many ways, inadvertently. But whatever it was, Sam didn't want any part in it. He simply decided to be as open as possible and offer as much assistance as he could. That way, he hoped he could soon put all this behind him.

Sam would never have associated JV with a homicide investigation in any context.

Financial or securities fraud, maybe, but homicide?

"Mr. Nathan, how long have you been in finance?" asked Alberts, glancing at him in the mirror.

"Twenty-one years or so. Honestly, I can't believe it's been that long. Time flies by when you are not looking. What is that popular saying, now? 'Time flies when you are having fun.' Well, I can't say that life has been all fun and games for me thus far, Detective Alberts, but the time has flown by in a heartbeat. Why am I being taken to the police station? I have no idea how I can help."

Sam stopped himself from uttering another word. He knew he was advised not to talk to the detectives. But he was nervous, and he couldn't stand the silence in the fast-moving car.

Morales was staring directly at the road ahead and asked, "Mr. Nathan, just how long have you known Mr. Jay Vishy? Does it surprise you that he had wiped out all his contacts from his phone? No family, no friends, just you, all by yourself on his list. So, I mean either he was extremely introverted and knew only you, or he deleted them all systematically."

It was as perplexing to Sam as to the officers. It was bizarre enough to think that Jay Vishy had somehow found his private unlisted number—but it was even more peculiar to now hear how Sam's number was the only contact stored. Why on earth would that be?

He answered openly, "I knew him only for the four years we were attending university together, and in fact, I haven't heard from him since we graduated in 1985. On occasion, I thought of him but not anytime recently. You know how life goes; you get busy, and it just flies by, all good intentions to stay in touch with college friends soon falling by the wayside. It isn't a deliberate thing, you understand. After college, the reality that is real life sets in, and you feel yourself getting drowned in your own rat race. The life we have as students does not emulate reality much.

"So, those college friends, as vital as they seemed at the time, no longer seem to have a place in the outside world. Weeks become years and years become decades. Before long, twenty years have passed, and the life you have now is no longer relevant to what happened way back when.

"But yes, I knew him very well back then. You could have called us best friends during those four years and wouldn't have been wrong. For the past twenty odd years, however, I have not been in touch with him once and have no idea how he got my number. Before you ask, yes, I guess I still consider him my friend and it may sound strange, but had we run into each other on the streets of LA, I think we would have carried on as if no time had passed since the last time we were together. Even though that was in another world, at another time. And despite us living our own completely separate and different lives today."

Sam was talking and talking, rarely a pause sufficient to draw breath. Alberts was still eyeing him in the rearview mirror, her forehead crinkled to a furrow as if deeply skeptical. Indeed, she was. Detectives knew that usually, when someone talked as effusively as this, they were covering up. Sam was just trying to control his nervousness and uneasiness.

Alberts and Morales were taking turns in asking questions.

"If that is true, why are you his only contact on his phone? Frankly, it makes no sense to me. Does it to you? Mr. Nathan."

Morales sounded suspicious, and Sam didn't appreciate his snide tone. Why didn't they ask JV himself about the contents of his phone?

Perhaps JV was the victim of a homicide, or maybe the suspect. Or maybe JV is missing. Yes, that must be it. It would be so like JV. After all, Sam knew JV to go missing for days on end. His gut lurched. Might these cops consider him, Sam, to have potentially played a role in a killing? He felt sick. He didn't appreciate being kept in the dark but stuck to his original plan of being as helpful as possible. But only in the presence of Gallagher. Sam kept going back to the fact that he was not in handcuffs, nor was he read his rights. He couldn't wait to see Gallagher.

You must definitely not be a suspect. You have done nothing wrong.

You know who you are and what you've done ... and not done, in this case. Just be honest, and they can't pin anything on you because there is nothing to pin. You haven't done anything!

Alberts also studied Sam through the rear-view mirror. He met her gaze with equally intent eyes and said, "I have no clue as to why JV would save only my contact on his phone. He was never a part of my life here."

Their car pulled up and parked in a space marked *Reserved* at the police station.

Alberts got out of the car as did Morales and Sam. She said, "You can come in and wait for Mr. Gallagher in my office."

As it turned out Jack Galagher was already at the police station. Jane Nolan must have impressed upon Gallagher of the seriousness and urgency of the matter, thought Sam, thanking his lucky stars for the pull Jane had. Gallagher looked experienced, probably in his late fifties or early sixties, with salt-and-pepper curly hair, black rimmed heavy glasses indicating a steel-trap mind in that head. A sharply dressed attorney in a dark blue suit and a red tie, he reached his hand to Sam and introduced himself, "Mr. Nathan. Jack Gallagher. Unfortunate circumstances bring us together. But your New York firm's legal counsel, Jane Nolan, and I go back a long time. I have known Jane for over forty years. She is a really sharp one."

From the looks of the expression on both Alberts and Morales they seemed to have encountered Gallagher before in their prior cases. Los Angeles was a big yet a small town. Important people knew other important people, not much different than New York City thought Sam. Gallagher nodded towards the detectives with a smile, and everyone moved in to Alberts office and sat down.

Gallagher addressed the detectives, "Detectives, I am representing Mr. Nathan. I want you to know that Mr. Nathan is here voluntarily and is willing to cooperate with you fully as long as you are forthright and completely open about what this is all about. I am his attorney of record. And what is that you need Mr. Nathan to answer? If I suspect a game being played here or if you are trying to entrap Mr. Nathan into admitting something he is not involved in, we are just getting up and walking out of here."

Alberts nodded and explained, "Mr. Gallagher, we assure you that Mr. Nathan is not a suspect in any investigation. We are only interested in speaking to him because he is the sole link we have to Mr. Vishy's past. We are seeking information about Mr. Vishy. We want to find out about Mr. Vishy's mental state and his way of thinking. We think that due to the unique connection Mr. Nathan had with Jay Vishy, he would be able to offer us an insight that not many others can."

Gallagher nodded and indicated that the detectives could proceed.

Alberts nodded and then she pulled out a big stack of photographs. She placed the stack upside down so only the white backs of the photos would show. They are large sized photos, thought Sam.

Morales started the questioning. And he had taken onto himself to address Sam with his first name.

"All right, Sam, perhaps we can start with you telling me the last time you spoke to Mr. Vishy."

Sam shook his head and didn't have to think hard.

"Definitely in 1985. I already told you that I haven't seen him since then."

Alberts seemed surprised at the exact same answer. She maintained her professional look, but Sam could see a measure of disbelief in her eyes. "You haven't spoken to Mr. Vishy in twenty-three years? Then why does he have your phone number on his phone? He has no other contacts. Why would he do that, why keep just you on there? Does that make any sense?"

"I already told you and Detective Morales what I know. You are asking the same questions and looking for different answers. Why don't you ask him yourself?" Sam blurted out. He was trying to be helpful and patient, but it wasn't easy with the same questions over and over, and why all that rush back at the hotel if they were just going to have him sitting here like this asking the same questions?

Alberts did nothing to relieve his rising tension. She said, "We have to ask these questions for the record in the presence of your attorney," when she suddenly grabbed his arm.

And pointed to a photo she had placed on the table. The big pile of photos was still turned upside down and in front of her. This was just the first photo she turned over and disclosed its full view for everyone at the table to see.

In the photo there was a body on the floor of a kitchen. It was obvious to Sam that the person, a woman, lay dead. His knees felt weak. He tried not to look closely but it appeared she had been shot in the head. He could hear Gallagher catch his breath and then start breathing deeply beside him. In contrast, Sam seemed surprisingly still.

"Did you know Mrs. Vishy?" Alberts asked him as she pointed to the body in the photo.

Sam could barely shake his head.

He mumbled, "No. Never seen her, never met her, never spoken to her. Didn't even know there was a Mrs. Vishy. He obviously got married at some point in time. How long ago did he get married to her?"

Sam was single and married life was not for him. It was just as impossible for him to imagine the JV he had known being married either. He hadn't seemed to be the settling down type when he was younger. Especially, given how private JV was and how frequently he would disappear mysteriously for days. JV wasn't the sharing kind. But a spouse being shot couldn't be an easy trauma to overcome for anyone.

He felt for JV and what he must be going through.

"Where is JV? If he thinks I am his friend, then perhaps I ought to behave like one."

What he meant by that was that if they could take him to JV, he could offer support. Right now, he didn't even care that the comment could be misconstrued and sound as if they were in contact.

Alberts didn't answer. She cast her eyes across to Morales, who nodded. Alberts pulled out the next photo from the pile of photos in her hand and turned it over displaying the color photo and pointed at the photo which showed another body, this time it was in a bedroom. This one was lying on a bed and seemed to be an elderly woman.

Sam leaned in to see her face. Alberts asked, "Did you know this woman?"

"No. Who is she? What happened to her?"

"She was shot in her sleep. In her head. One shot. Whoever did this, they did it very efficiently," said Alberts. "She was Mrs. Angelie Vishy's mother. Mr. Vishy's mother-in-law."

The sight of blood was getting to Sam. He was not good with blood, never had been. That was one of the reasons he had ruled out studying medicine long back when he was in high school. Dissecting a frog in high school biology class was something he had done reluctantly and with extreme disgust. The natural ease with numbers led him to pursue engineering like countless others of his age in India. He could handle it if it was his own blood as he'd had his own fair share of injuries and accidents through the years in sports and other activities, but he could never handle blood when it was from others.

Sam glanced at Gallagher sitting next to him. Gallagher seemed to be calm and looked quite resolute. Some how it seemed like he was trying to infuse strength into Sam.

Morales addressed Alberts, saying, "I think he's able to handle the crime scene in its entirety. Let us show him the other photos now and see if he can shed some light on that."

Sam had a foreboding of worse to come if that were even possible. He wanted to interject that now, he couldn't handle any more, and this was already more than enough, tormenting him.

The two detectives were very matter of fact and detached.

Sam supposed they had to be this way in their line of work where they would see these things all the time. But it was getting to be too much for him. He was feeling as though time stood still and at the same time, that he was speeding forward much too fast. He was aware that now Alberts had placed a set of three more photos of yet another bedroom, a teenager's room, maybe a college freshman or sophomore. The three photos together painted an overall picture in Sam's mind.

The kid had clearly been an artist, the room chock full of art supplies and drawings everywhere.

Sam struggled to look at this young man's face and turned away quickly.

He had been shot in the left temple, seemingly also as he'd been sleeping. He looked all of eighteen years old. The killer had to have been looking straight at him and placed the gun close to the kid's temple when he'd shot him. The teen looked peaceful, as if he had just drifted into a nice slumber, bringing pleasant dreams. One of his eyes was not fully closed showing a narrow sliver of the whites of his eye somehow highlighting his dark eyelashes, and there was blood from his right ear, soaking the pillow.

It was a strange thought that passed through Sam's mind when he considered *there is not as much blood as I'd have imagined, considering how many killings.* But the thing about a shooting was that the heart soon stopped sending a victim's vital ruby life force around the body.

It was the still pumping heart that ensured murder scenes became doused in blood. With fatal shootings, there was usually one major escape of blood, then nothing, small trails congealing.

This scene was cold and brutal. This poor boy, this talented boy, had obviously been JV's son.

Despite the shocking scene, Sam couldn't help but appreciate the extraordinary art in the room. He noticed a beautiful painting of Kobe Bryant, the Los Angeles Lakers basketball legend.

Various UCLA Bruins merchandise decorated the room too, from T-shirts and pennants to mugs and some autographed pictures and giant wall posters.

Sam recognized Coach Wooden's photo on the door of the young man's closet. John Wooden was a legendary basketball coach who had led UCLA to ten national basketball championships. This kid seemed to be an artist and a basketball fan, not to mention an UCLA Bruin.

Sam's mind was turning to butter, and he felt cold and hot all at the same time. From somewhere far away, he heard Morales asking questions like a distant echo. "Have you seen this young man before? Did you know JV was married and had a boy who was a freshman at UCLA?" Sam could barely stay focused. He sat there, almost in a trance, marveling at this kid's artistic skills.

He felt so sad to see such a promising young life snuffed out so coldly.

Detective Morales noticed Sam's discomfort and passed him a small unopened bottle of cold water. He took a sip and tried to gather himself. Taking a deep breath, he said he had not known anything about JV's son let alone that he had a son.

Sam now was getting ready to stand up, thinking they were done, more likely wishing they were done. But Detective Alberts took him by the arm and began to pull him down to force him into his chair. Sam turned to Gallagher and Gallagher looked at Sam and just nodded with an intense look in his eye. The next set of photos were of another bedroom. Sam didn't want to see any more.

He had already seen more horrors in a few minutes than he had witnessed in his entire life.

He sat back in his chair closing his eyes.

His knees were weak, and he felt sick to his stomach. Alberts wouldn't take no for an answer though, coaxing him to open his eyes and look. And there it was. This was the ultimate shocker. He heard Gallagher take a gulp sitting next to him. It was another bedroom, this time belonging to two younger kids, both boys, one on either side of the room, on each of their own beds. Blood all over the sheets. They had been shot in the head like the others.

And there in between them, sitting on a chair was his old friend JV, a gun still barely in his hand. Barefoot and dressed in a blue

UCLA Bruins T-shirt and jeans, he was slumped down and facing to his left. A bullet wound on the right side of his forehead was still wet with blood.

He looked the same, only older, his face having gotten really gaunt and sunken.

He'd had a much fuller face back in IIT. Sam should have expected this based on what he'd seen already in the other photos and the ones being displayed now on the table, but he hadn't seen this coming at all.

After all these years, this is how he ended it? Why couldn't he have done this in IIT like the others who did in our four years there? Why did he have to take all these other innocent lives with him? Should I have known? Could I have helped? But, no—I didn't know the guy. Not any longer. This was as much a stranger to me as to the detectives.

For the first time in twenty-three years, Sam felt that same old suffocating feeling that he'd often felt in his four years at that hellhole. He had forgotten how intensely suffocating that feeling had been.

JV had left that hellhole with Sam, but it looked as if the hell had never left JV. It had stayed with him with an iron grip, not letting go until it took him. This time, hell had been made to wait so long that it had gathered enough rage and despondency to take five others as well, stealing away the closest five people who had nothing to do with anything. JV had fought long and hard and the longer he had fought, the harder he had fought, the stronger the isolation had grown, the stronger the despondency, the stronger the wastefulness. The deeper the hell. The years and years when this hell inside of him had lain dormant, it was just waiting and building strength, waiting for the right time to erupt. Like a volcano, the eruption was sudden, violent, explosive and shockingly unexpected.

It would have been so much better for him to have given in, early on in his freshman year.

What was for many a beautiful mild southern California day, turned out to be the ugliest of Sam's life. The pit in his stomach resurfaced so many times. He had to find a way to get past this.

His finance background had trained him to always look to the next trade; in finance, a person was required to have a short memory. Whether a trade was a winner or loser, it didn't matter, you had to move on to the next. That training told Sam that he needed to get through this and onto the next day, and he had to find a way to put this day, the absolute worst of his life, far behind him.

Gallagher suggested that perhaps Sam should fill in the detectives with everything he knew about JV from his days at IIT without holding anything back so he could then escort Sam out of the police station. It would shed light on JV's personality for the detectives, thought Gallagher.

The detectives had agreed and asked him to go back in time and tell them the entire four years' experience with this man, this mass murderer as they saw it, JV. They were looking for clues, hints about why a man like this would suddenly blow out the brains of his dear family. In cold blood and ruthlessly.

As Sam finished with the part about them getting their student visas in June, 1985, Alberts ended with, "What a sad story! I thought that college days were supposed to be the best years!"

Morales chimed in with his own wisdom. "Says who? The colleges? Why do you think they charge you so much for tuition? Why do you think there are so many colleges everywhere? It's nothing but a money-making machine, partner. What else are they going to say? 'Send us your kids, give us your money and we will turn them into mental cases?' Boy, am I glad my son is working straight out of high school! At least he's doing something he loves, right off the bat."

Deep inside, Sam gave Morales props. He had a very practical view, but IIT was actually free for those who got in. It wasn't about money for IIT; it was to develop the future engineers of the world. But the system was out of whack, that much was true, and the road to that particular hell was paved with good intentions. Students there didn't learn what they were supposed to, instead learning what they were not supposed to. And maybe there was some truth in Morales' observation.

Almost everything useful was acquired by learning on the job; people learned best by doing, not by cramming for tests. Sam was as good an example as there could ever be. Nothing they had ever taught him at that hellhole had proved to be of any use to him in 'real life', quite frankly. The gift with numbers was genetic, perhaps handed down from his own father's gift with numbers.

He had come to learn so much more outside of the classroom than in them at IIT. The life-coping skills he had managed to pick up on his own through his own experiences helped him a lot more. JV's presence with his continuous supply of Amitabh magic had helped him cope with mental pressures. In due time, Sam had learned to find ways of coping with all kinds of pressure situations.

The ability to stay calm under pressure ended up helping Sam in his career in finance.

In the end, every door any person would open was just a pathway to open more doors.

Each door by itself didn't help much; the only usefulness came when a series of the right doors opened up all at the right time. Somehow, for Sam, the doors opened up one after another and he found himself on the doorstep of horror that day.

Gallagher and Sam got up to leave. Sam didn't remember much about the walk back to Gallagher's car. Gallagher had offered to drive Sam back to his hotel suite.

Once back at his hotel, Sam headed for the shower to get ready for his afternoon meeting in Marina del Rey with his client. Which was the reason for Sam's visit to Los Angeles in the first place, until this JV situation threw everything for a loop.

Chapter Seven:

The Aftermath

That evening as Sam was going over his notes on the successful appointment in Marina del Rey that he had managed to keep, his phone rang. *Damn it, I need to change that annoying ringtone,* he thought once again as he answered. Each time that wretched device set off ringing, he would have that same thought.

It was Jack Gallagher. Jack said that there was a gathering of a bunch of friends of JV and Angelie's at the club house in JV's neighborhood and wondered if Sam would like to go. It was just an informal get together to remember Angelie, JV, and the kids. Jack said he came to know about it from a news reporter who had contacted Gallagher for a comment about the murders. Declining to comment, Gallagher had thereafter spoken to the lady who had arranged the gathering and found out it was open to anyone who wished to attend. Sam was not inclined for company, especially a crowded company. Gallagher said that it might do some good to be with others who knew Angelie and JV instead of spending the evening alone. Sam thanked Gallagher and politely declined.

A few minutes later that phone rang again. Sam was getting perturbed. He kept forgetting to change the ring tone.

"Mr. Nathan? Mr. Nathan, this is Sylvia Nelson. I got your number from Jack Gallagher. I hope you don't mind my calling. I am… well, I was Angelie and JV's next-door neighbor. Please, I know this is a big ask, but would you be able to come and spend a few minutes with us, me, and my husband? We want to talk to you about JV and his family and I take it that you knew him well from the way Jack Gallagher talked about you. I just finished talking to Jack myself and he suggested I call you as you had a story to tell about JV. There's so much unanswered here. We're all so devastated."

Why did Gallagher go and give out my number without asking? The call had surprised Sam but upon hearing Sylvia's plea in her voice, he decided he had no reason not to meet Sylvia and her husband. This was a terrible day, and those who did not know much about JV would never be able to understand the tragedy. Sam had only known him for a short period of time so long ago, and despite knowing some of the hidden demons JV was carrying, he couldn't understand what had happened either. Maybe talking to Sylvia could help them both piece together what had led to these dreadful events.

And as people said, *A problem shared is a problem halved.* Or so he dearly hoped.

To avoid the long drive, they agreed to meet about halfway in between at a diner later that night.

When Sam walked in, he saw a woman he assumed to be Sylvia sitting at a corner table by herself. She motioned to him to join her at her table. Her husband couldn't join them as he had some issue at his office with his work being held up late. He was in finance also, so it was just as well that he didn't show up as Sam didn't want to be talking shop.

This was supposed to be all about JV and finding a way to come to terms with and even getting past this experience. It had been a very long day, one which Sam just wished would end.

"Thank you for meeting me, Mr. Nathan. I know how terrible a day it's been for you, as it has been for us, his neighbors. Such a horrible, dreadful shock for us all."

"Please call me Sam. Yes, it has been an awful day for us all. I hope that you can find a way to get through this," Sam replied, meaning every word as the anguish showed on both their faces.

"It is so sad, so, so sad. What a nice family and such a waste. I am devastated. Angelie was such a beautiful person, you know, Sam. We worked together; you know. We are both nurses at the hospital. Sorry, Angelie *was* a nurse also. I can't even start to get to grips with this. And the kids, the kids … Those poor children." She had tears in her eyes. Sam motioned to the server and offered the woman a napkin that he pulled from the dispenser on the table.

Sam asked the waitress for cold water and additional napkins.

Sylvia sniffed into the napkin loudly and continued, "Angelie, she was never late for work. Today, I mean yesterday, I've lost track of time, she just didn't show up at all, which isn't like her. So, I called her and called her but got no response. Then I asked for an extended break at the hospital and went to check on her. I drove back to our neighborhood and to Angelie's place. The newspaper was still on the front porch! Something was wrong. Both their cars were still in the driveway, and their front door was unlocked and slightly ajar. The door was open, Sam, as if JV wanted me to just walk in on the horror. How terrible!

"Last night, or…umm… the night before, when I was returning from work, I saw JV outside shooting baskets on his driveway with his sons, I waved at him. You know what he said to me? He pulled me aside out of earshot of his kids and warned that there were burglaries in the neighborhood. And that I should keep my windows shut at night."

She was dabbing at her eyes as she gathered her composure.

"He said I should even close my windows upstairs, the ones facing the children's bedrooms of his house. He had this all planned out; he knew that was the last time he would be shooting baskets with his sons. He clearly didn't want me to hear the gunshots. Unbelievably awful!"

Sam wasn't altogether surprised by this revelation and gave Sylvia a little insight into JV's mind. "JV was a genius and unfortunately, he used his smarts to plan this horrific ending. I feel for you, Sylvia. I only knew JV a long time ago when he and I were young. We were friends in college. He was always quite mysterious and unpredictable, but he always knew what he wanted to do. It was a bad combination, a genius but tortured mind and a knack to plan things out."

She nodded and continued, "He seemed quite happy financially. When he moved in a year or so ago, he told me he was renting this house because he'd made a big profit on selling his previous one; he was still thinking about where to invest all the money he'd made.

"But Detective Morales said that it was probably financial stress. I don't understand it. Such a beautiful family. So sad. She wasn't very social but she was great with her kids. He was so loving to his sons too, always hugging and kissing them on their cheeks. Such a waste."

After a small pause, Sylvia asked, "What can you tell me about JV? What do you think could have led him to this? How long did you know him?"

Sam sighed deeply. "Do you ever watch any Bollywood movies?" he wanted to know.

She shook her head, and he sat there thinking for a moment as to how to convey the deep fandom JV had for Amitabh and how in a roundabout way Amitabh had helped save JV and Sam years ago. There were no parallels in Hollywood to Amitabh. And the cultural differences would make it so hard for Sylvia to understand the magic of Amitabh Bachchan.

"The complicated part of this story is that it spreads across two immensely different worlds. It would be almost impossible to encapsulate all there is to cover. How much time do you have?"

They ended up talking for almost two hours, with Sam doing most of the speaking and Sylvia mostly asking questions. He let her have the entire story from the moment he'd met JV, to the final moment of seeing him over twenty years ago. It didn't answer any particular questions for her but Sam thought she seemed calmer on learning all about JV in his younger days. Maybe just talking helped her calm down. Sam found that retelling and reliving the moments with JV somehow helped him cope as well.

As the conversation moved to small talk about the time and the journey, they got up to leave, Sylvia shook Sam's hand, looked into his eyes and said, "Take care of yourself, ok?"

As Sam got into his car and drove away from the parking lot of the diner, Sylvia was still standing by her car, waving at him. He waved back.

As he was driving back, Sam thought that Gallagher's decision of releasing his phone number to Sylvia was actually a good thing as Sam felt much better after talking to someone unaffiliated with law enforcement. It felt like an emotional release since it was a normal conversation rather than an interrogation.

Back at the hotel, Sam was checking some of his papers in his briefcase and remembered that the detectives had rifled through his briefcase. Gallagher had been fine with it, stating that Sam had nothing to hide. Sam saw his New York firm's brochure in the pocket of the briefcase. New York seemed so far away. *Well, damn. I'll have to call Gallagher tomorrow and see if I can fly back to New York now. Surely the cops are done with me.*

He pondered on this tragedy. It seemed pretty black and white, so what was the need for an investigation, especially one requiring the presence of a man who'd had no part in the lives of those involved? He poured himself a drink from the suite's bar as he wouldn't be going out again that night. *And what about all of JV's writings? He was such a great writer ... He should have been an author, not bothering about going into investments. Such a waste. It's all come to nothing.*

He smiled to himself, losing himself momentarily in reverie, slightly saddened at the thought of what had become of JV and his loving family. The funny incident of JV's lost room key flooded back into his mind. He was so strange about money matters that spending one penny was too much, even if it would help him to save a dollar! *But then again, we are all different.*

JV had never had the gift of making financial decisions. That much was not JV's fault.

But why did he stray so far from his gift, his talent and love for writing?

Why go into something he so clearly had no disposition for? Nor was it where his natural gift was.

On leaving Columbia with his master's degree, Sam himself had been a bit of a Johnny-come-lately, with no clear idea of where he could get a job. He had ended up doing a bit of writing too early on, just prior he had landed his first full-time job.

But Sam's writing was for only a few weeks and was about financial issues, U.S treasury bond price movements and about potential trades, entirely factual, nowhere near the level of JV's poetic skill with words. And Sam was dealing in finance which JV had ended up doing too, yet Sam was the one who had been good at it. One foot here, one foot there. Somehow, he had found a balance that JV evidently hadn't. He had managed to get out and survive, while JV hadn't found a route to doing that for himself for whatever reason. The talented and superior mind had succumbed, the mediocre one surviving.

Now, Sam had to dig deep and find a way to put this behind him once and for all.

For his own sanity.

Chapter Eight:

The Morning After

Next morning at breakfast, Sam sat at the table for a while and read the newspapers as he often would. One of them was carrying a story about JV, unsurprising really, given the horrific nature of the murders. Yet it was a dry, matter-of-fact narrative without any attempt at an explanation of the tragedy or background that might have led him to commit such atrocities.

His breakfast was interrupted by a phone call from Jack Gallagher. Jack had beaten him to the phone call he had intended to make. Gallagher had managed to get a copy of some files from the detectives along with an envelope marked for Sam. Gallagher invited Sam to come over to his office in Santa Monica to look at the files the detectives had handed to Gallagher for Sam to take a look. Not being that far from his hotel, Sam made it to Gallagher's office promptly. Avoiding the freeways had helped with the quick drive.

"These are some financial records that JV kept. Perhaps it will help you make sense of what happened. The cops have closed the case now. It has been ruled a murder suicide. There is nothing that they wanted you for aside from some information. They appreciated your cooperation."

Gallagher pulled a chair for Sam at the conference room table. Then he parked himself next to Sam and asked if there was anything that made any sense in the files. Sam scanned through the first few pages and started to develop his interpretation of what he saw. Sam seemed to be talking to himself with Gallagher sitting next to him, absorbing everything.

"JV graduated from UCLA in 1987 and somehow found himself working at Sony Pictures. Several years later, he'd started a venture fund around the time that the dot-com market had begun exhibiting early signs of instability in the year 2000.

"There are hardly any papers about this particular venture in the folder, but from what is there, it seems to have been a venture fund based out of London, UK. As one of the founders, JV was allocated some warrants. I don't know if you understand what these warrants are?"

Gallagher nodded, but he said, "Perhaps you'd explain it to me anyway."

"Well, they are an option to buy a stock at a predetermined price and they're used as an incentive to invite investors or owners to put money into the venture at a key point in time."

To explain to Gallagher in simple language, Sam used an example.

Since JV had put in around $15,000 into that venture fund, Sam made up some hypothetical numbers to show the way it could have worked.

"Suppose JV was given warrants allowing him to buy 20,000 shares of this venture called NanoV as a reward for the $15,000 he'd already invested. Working under this assumption, the $15,000 investment gave JV the 'rights' to buy twenty thousand shares at preset price of $1 each.

"This was during the end of the dot-com bull market, which had topped off in 2000. Clearly, JV was brilliant, and he would have seen the bear market coming; in fact, the bear had already been ravaging stock trading accounts by the time 2001 rolled around. At some point, he would have seen that the price of the stock for NanoV had risen all the way up to $90 a share from the teens, then had started coming down again. When it kept going down and hit around $60, he exercised his warrants, buying up the twenty thousand shares he had the right to buy at $1 each, and he turned around and sold them immediately for $60 a share, walking away with $1.2 million. So, he had put in an initial $15,000. And then an additional $20,000 to buy the stock at $1 each. And walked away with $1.2 million. JV had miraculously turned $35,000 to $1.2 million."

At this point, Gallagher widened his eyes and urged Sam to continue.

The files contained a clipping from a British newspaper in which the reporter had written about JV's profits from the NanoV venture. From what Sam could see, this had been JV's first foray into investments. By happenstance, he had also discovered that his first money venture outside of his normal work had yielded a fantastic return, especially impressive since this happened as most accounts were getting hit or were about to get hit by a serious bear market across all financial markets around the world. When everybody around him was losing money, JV made a killing.

Sam could only imagine how elated he would have been. No doubt it had boosted his self-confidence as an investor. In turn, it only led him to casually try his hand at a few other ventures, but he never entered anything of consequence with any significant sum of his NanoV profits.

To Sam's eyes, it looked like a lot of curious probing without any serious commitment.

Most of the records in the files were missing papers and were thus incomplete, and due to this, it was hard to understand the thinking behind JV's approach. Sam didn't see a disciplined investor with a specific methodology at play; rather, he saw a lot of darts being thrown randomly at the board, hoping something would land. More hope than proper decision making.

This undisciplined method was a recurring pattern until 2006 when JV sold his home. Sam later found out the details of his home-selling process too. Again, JV had shown he was astute in his observations, evidently having noticed that a few houses in his neighborhood had started popping up with 'for sale' signs. He wasn't going to wait. He knocked on his neighbor's door, and his neighbor, Jackie McKinley, was a real estate agent.

He had seen Jackie's face on many home sale signs around his neighborhood.

Jackie answered the door, saying, "Hey neighbor! How are you? What's going on?"

"Hi Jackie. Good morning. How are you? So many homes around the neighborhood have your name and face on the signs!" replied JV.

"Well, it looks like a lot of people are upgrading and moving up the price scale. People have made good money on their homes over the past ten years or so." Jackie smiled.

JV started pacing back and forth, muttering nonsensical things to himself for a couple of minutes. Then he stopped, looked at Jackie and said, "So, just incidentally, what would you think my house would fetch in the market if I sold it today?"

Jackie was used to JV's bluntness from their prior interactions in the neighborhood, and said, "Well, without doing an appraisal, I wouldn't be able to pinpoint an exact figure, but I would say maybe around a million? Give or take. Somewhere in that ballpark. It has been taking eighteen to thirty-five days to move houses in this neighborhood. That is a very fast-moving inventory. If you wait a couple of months, you may get a higher price as the market is still rising."

JV shook his head and said, "Would you be interested in selling my house?"

Soon, JV had his house on the market, and it sold within a month. This whole house-selling thing had been a point of contention between JV and his wife. Angelie didn't want to move.

His wife had always prized comfort above wealth, and any potential gains by moving homes right now would be overshadowed by the hassle factor of the move and the personal losses incurred by doing so. For one thing, she had friends and colleagues from work who lived close by, and the kids had friends they considered very close just down the road. Because of their happy, close-knit little community, she perceived this was one reason—but a major one—for why the kids were doing so well at school. They were settled. They all felt secure, and it showed in so many ways.

JV was having none of it. In fact, he didn't even want to buy a new house after this one sold.

He had paid around $250,000 for their house in 1997 and he wanted to hang on to the three-quarters of a million dollars in profit he would have made by selling it.

JV ended up renting a home a few miles away in a different school district.

This of course meant changing schools for the kids and making new acquaintances with the new neighbors. Moving was a headache, which it always is, no matter the purported benefits. Angelie moved reluctantly, believing that a profit of $750,000 was not worth uprooting her life for. They had enough money already, funds to get by day to day, to live a more than comfortable life. There was only one go at this life too, she believed, and accruing three quarters of a million dollars meant what? They could not take their newfound affluence with them when they departed this world, but happy memories and a lifetime of stability, they could take those things, and rest easy.

What would be the advantage to selling up now, uprooting their stability and familiarity?

But there was no arguing with JV once he made up his mind. Sam knew that all too well. There would have been no—or very few—discussions around the matter. JV was always a leader, and he would have carried that into his own household. At least, he was not a leader of men in the traditional way, yet he was one who could not be swayed; he knew what he wanted and took it.

Sure enough, the files showed that a couple of months later, JV checked his old house's market value and was struck to find it had gone up now to $1.5 million dollars.

There was a printout of the new valuation and JV had written 'TOO SOON' in block capitals across it. Additional notes showed all this was bothering him quite a bit. He was upset that he had sold his house too soon and if only he had heeded Jackie McKinley's observation that waiting a bit would fetch a higher price. Not just any higher price but half-a-million dollars higher!

It was after JV moved to the rental house that Sam first noticed the signs of distress in his trading account. For whatever reason, JV had accumulated shares of a big Fortune 500 insurance company named AIG. It was a very liquid stock at that time, trading over 500,000 shares each day with an average price of over $1,000 per share. He had bought 2100 shares or close to two million dollars' worth of AIG stock with an average price of $950. In other words, it was everything he had.

Sam couldn't figure out why he would have been going 'all in' on one stock.

The truth was that initially, it looked like a sound investment as the stock went up as high as $1450 in the middle of 2007 from his purchase price of $950.

At this point, his stock holdings would have been worth over three million dollars.

Sam knew very well from personal experience what a successful trade felt like.

You felt as though you were the smartest guy on the planet, totally invincible. It was a better feeling but in fact a worse scenario than winning in Vegas. In Las Vegas, you would at least be holding chips and the dollar figure would not be staring at you all the time during the play.

When you are trading, you can clearly see everything on your computer monitor: your initial investment; the buy price; the current price; and the current account value.

Sam imagined JV staring at his account that had been worth two million dollars as it rapidly grew to a value of three million in a matter of months.

Was he on there every day, ogling the screen? Most probably. Knowing JV's mental make-up, Sam doubted he would have been tempted to sell, even though it would have been a good time to do so. If Sam had known JV back then, however, and if he'd been aware of what he was doing, he would have advised him to sell. That advice could very well have fallen on deaf ears though. From the files, Sam could tell that JV was still aloof, cocky, and super confident in his own abilities.

But the stock market comes to bite many smart people, history being replete with tales of those who made millions only to lose it all again in what seemed to be the blink of an eye.

Ego almost always comes into play and the conviction of being right becomes so strong that the most sensible decision is rarely made. This pattern is seen in the very smallest of wins; a person winning ten dollars on a lottery scratch card usually buys another scratch card with their winnings, and if they win again, they do it again. And so it goes on, the wish to be lucky.

The belief in the universe providing something from nothing. Sometimes, the universe treats someone graciously and kindly, but you can bet your bottom dollar it also snatches back any wins.

Sure enough, as the housing market turned sour, AIG started its historic slide in prices.

Sam wasn't privy to the daily and weekly stresses that JV felt.

The new year, 2008, had begun with a lot of turmoil in the stock market.

Sam noticed a handwritten note in JV's handwriting on the side of his trading records, relating to early February 2008. It read, "Oh, my God, I lost all of the one million profit I had!"

AIG's price had fallen back to around JV's original purchase price of $950 from its high of $1450, promptly dropping his account value from three million back to its original value of two million dollars. A month later, AIG's price further slid down to $800 and now, his account was worth $1.6 million, representing a paper loss of $400,000 on his original two million dollars.

Of course, he believed that pulling back in a panic was not usually the best course of action. Leave the investment sitting there, and in time, it would rise again.

Selling on a whim, JV must have thought, could be tantamount to financial suicide.

But JV's notes indicated to Sam that he was getting more than nervous.

There was another note sitting there at this point in the records, however, one about his experience with the sale of his home, and how he had sold it too early. It may have been the seed sprouting his reluctance to sell his AIG stock holdings. He was going to hold onto them a while.

Impatience had cost him before, and he seemed agitated that it would do so again.

Sam got the feeling that JV's prior experiences of wins in the stock market had been purely by chance. He was astute in some respects, but he just didn't have in place the automatic mechanisms a successful trader used. If his account was up a million dollars, at the very least, a normal trader would have placed a sell-stop if the profit were to drop from a million dollars to half a million.

By doing this, the trader walked away with at least half a million in profits.

A stop—being an automatic selling order placed at a predetermined price should the stock fall to a certain price— could have saved him. For example, he could have placed a sell-stop at $1200 and when AIG went from $1450 to $1200 on its way down to $800, he would have been sold out at $1200, and still walked away with his five hundred thousand gain, not a bad outcome at all.

The pressure he was feeling in March 2008 seemed to alleviate marginally in late April of 2008, just six weeks later, when AIG rebounded from $800, heading back up almost to $1000.

At this point, he was no longer facing a loss, but then began the real stress and financial distress.

This scenario now had Sam puzzled; why was JV still intent on holding the stock? He knew that JV was cocky and considered himself smarter than the rest, and Sam suspected that his experience of selling his home too early may have played a more than incidental role in it.

JV was also smarter than most for sure, but he was not the smartest of all.

He perhaps also never grasped that the market was not about being smart or brilliant.

The market was always about protecting yourself against the worst outcomes. Sam knew that JV didn't possess the basic traits of a successful trader, which necessitated having a lack of ego, possessing humility, and an understanding that the market could and would do unthinkable things.

JV probably didn't think a $1450 stock would fall far. Especially when a label of *Fortune 500* is attached to the company.

The market, of course, had other ideas. By July 2008, within three months after seeing a price of around $1000, AIG had fallen to $500, and JV was now over a million dollars in the red. From being up a million, he had gone down by the same amount within a few months.

Sam saw desperation in the notes but incredibly, JV still held hope, one note proclaiming, "AIG fell from $1000 in late April to $500 in July. It's a Fortune 500. It will now definitely rebound!"

The files included clippings from financial papers such as Barron's and The Wall Street Journal, even Sam was feeling a knot in his stomach when he came across these. In his experience, it was never a good idea to pay attention to other people when dealing with the financial markets.

Seven billion people on the planet would have seven billion or more different opinions.

Then came September 2008. Now, in the early part of this month, AIG stock sat at $450.

JV's files contained even more clippings from financial newspapers, some saying that AIG would rebound soon as the housing crisis would be solved by the government. There were only clippings of reports saying the market would rebound because that was what he wanted to hear. Sam noticed there were no clippings of the opinions that claimed the market would tank. JV was only listening to what he desperately wanted to hear.

The rebound JV had been anticipating hadn't come yet.

His two million was about $950,000 now, a terrible slide.

But hope remained eternal, and he somehow kept his hope up even though his losses were mounting. His notes revealed that he hadn't uttered a single word to anyone, not even to his wife, Angelie. Then came the two most devastating weeks, back-to-back, one after another.

That next week, AIG was to plummet from $450 to $250, leaving JV stunned. His habitually neat writing had metamorphosed into a scribble that Sam couldn't even read.

And the following week was the final straw, AIG plunging as low as $25. His account that had once stood at three million dollars, was now worth only $50,000.

From what Sam could make out, he was in deep distress by now, and it was hardly surprising.

Another handwritten note referred to some stock analyst who claimed that AIG could totally collapse and be worth pennies quite soon. After all this time and all these losses, finally a clipping of the opposing opinion to his own! Sam concluded that this was what had convinced JV in the end, and the AIG stock price sat at a mere $40 when he liquidated his holdings. He had bought at $950 and sold at $40!

This was the ultimate act of desperation.

JV's account was now a mere $80,000, less than the sum he owed in debts. Sam could never comprehend how human beings believe just because a company is well-known, or a stock is priced over $1000 that it couldn't fall all the way down to pennies. It has been known to happen before; it will happen again in the future.

He could no longer afford to pay tuition for any of his younger kids' private schools, let alone his oldest son's UCLA costs. He was financially finished, total financial ruin, with a negative net worth. Sam closed the folder and pushed it back to the center of the table.

He stopped for a moment and looked at Gallagher.

He was paying rapt attention to Sam.

Gallagher slowly stood up and stared out of his office's third floor windows. It was yet another beautiful mild sunny day in greater Los Angeles. Sam's take about JV's financial actions had stunned even him, one who had seen plenty in the world of the well-to-do.

"Holy crap! From three million to eighty thousand? That would do me in too. No wonder he lost his mind. What a mess!"

Sam turned toward Gallagher and gathered his thoughts. Then he said in as calm a voice as he could manage, "You know, eighty-thousand dollars is quite frankly a lot of money and a good initial pool to start trading in stocks if you know what you are doing. I have seen many a successful trader turn amounts even less than that into a considerable fortune.

"It would have taken JV some time, of course, perhaps a handful of years or more, but he could have turned things around. All he had to do was buy time from his creditors and perhaps make certain adjustments to his lifestyle. Show some humility, take some responsibility, and even seek help from people he knew. Heck, if he had just called me, I would have done what I could to help him out. There was no shame in asking for help. I could have lent a helping hand …"

"Really? You'd have done that for him, even though you hadn't had contact for two decades?"

Gallagher asked, his head on one side, like he himself couldn't have offered a helping hand to one so irresponsible.

He seemed to appear skeptical. But it was what it was; as Sam's thoughts were, when two friends were close as JV and he had once been, they could bump into one another decades later and take up again exactly where they had left off. The years would not have intervened to separate them. They were buddies, and that was that. Yes, he would have helped. In Sam's mind, JV had rescued Sam in his own way during the depths of despair at IIT. Sam wouldn't have hesitated had the opportunity to help JV been offered.

"I know what you mean but college friends are always close if you understand. We could have crossed paths again at any time and picked up our friendship again as if we'd never been apart. It was that kind of friendship we had. But let's say he didn't want any direct help, then at least I could have guided him on some steps he could have taken to help him get through the current financial bind. In time, he would have recovered most, if not even more, of his financial status."

He mused on what he'd just said, then added, "And you will know as well as I do, that it's male pride that takes a hit. It's having to admit your failure to your wife, your family, your friends. But to be honest, if we had spoken about it, I probably would have lent him some funds and advised him to say nothing to anyone yet, just reinvesting for now. It really was not all that bad. It only felt that bad from where JV stood, and that was because he had started at three million and seen it slide. But to me, eighty thousand is a decent enough sum and a reasonable sum to rebuild with."

Sam felt frustrated that he could have prevented all of this. But JV would have had to ask and then been willing to accept help and advice from someone he had perhaps always considered to be of inferior intellect. In JV's eyes, everyone was of inferior intellect to his own. Sam sighed and continued to explain to Gallagher.

"These kinds of thoughts would have never occurred to JV. In his mind, he was the smartest and his family thought he was the definition of the American dream. His community also thought of him as a genius who made it. In his own eyes, his view of himself was something other than reality. JV could never have found it in him to reach out to me. But even if he couldn't reach out to me, he could have done so with anyone he considered a good friend. But

I doubt he had any good friends, and that must be why I was the only name in his address book, as sad as that makes me. So, you see, it was destined to end this way. There just wasn't any other way this could have ended."

Gallagher took the folder and put it away quietly, breathing heavily as if emotion gripped him.

Then he pulled out a manila envelope, placing both his hands on it.

He asked Sam, "Was your 3 p.m. client meeting yesterday with a gentleman representing an entity called *I-Squared Investments?*"

Sam couldn't hide his surprise. "Yes! How did you know that?"

Gallagher sat down and leaned back in his chair. "I was given copies of all these files you are looking at and this folder here in my hands by the detectives once they closed the case. I don't know how to tell you, but I-Squared Investments were hired by Mr. Vishy. He had hired them to contact you, and have you come to Los Angeles specifically on the day that he killed himself. It was a murder-suicide; JV killed everybody in that house including himself. As you can imagine, the financial stress was too much for him to handle."

Sam was speechless as Gallagher added, "He wanted you here for this, Sam. Don't ask me why. I suppose you were his only friend and whatever he thought of you, I cannot understand. If he considered you his sole friend, his ally, why would he want to put you through this heinous act?

"Why would he want you here to witness this deeply upsetting and traumatizing incident? I have seen some warped sickos in my time, but this one takes the cake, wouldn't you agree?"

Sam was silent, almost tearful, nodding in agreement. Why would JV have planned for that?

It was a despicable thing he had wanted to do to Sam. It would have ruined his life. God knew, the police officers having shown him the photos of the horrific scene of the crime was bad enough.

Gallagher went on, "As per the detectives, JV left a suicide note. It said he had thought of two possible options as a way out. The first option was just to kill himself. But, of course, that sicko couldn't do that because you know, his family's honor would have been in the dumpster if he'd done that. He would've thought of his wife finding out about his colossal financial failure and shortcomings as he saw it. His mode of thinking fits that of a narcissist perfectly; the narcissist or someone with narcissistic tendencies thinks of himself and his self-image and ego before anything else, even if he will not be alive anymore when the truth of his mistakes is uncovered. Such is the depth of their depraved thinking.

"He undoubtedly would have imagined the scenario in which his wife was told of his failures, and how she would have had to sit the kids down and tell them how they'd now have to economize. His pride could not handle anything of that sort. He had to be the best of the best, even in death.

"So, it was better to execute each one of them before taking his own life. Now, there is no family left behind to find him a failure or to be dishonored. But this happens all the time in murder-suicides where the perpetrator is the so-called head of the household, the supposed major breadwinner. It's a pattern we see often. What a gem of a nutcase, don't you think, Sam? This guy was something!"

Gallagher said, "Don't mind my insensitivity, Sam. It is not every day that even I, in my line of work, get to see this kind of execution. Yes, there are plenty of head-of-household murder-suicides seen by the police in general but I have seen none before in *my* legal cases. We could go crazy just trying to understand these hideous acts. JV had bought that handgun just recently. He had gone to great lengths to take shooting lessons. Detective Alberts said that the dates of his gun lessons seem to have coincided with the weeks of severe losses in his stock trading account that you've told me about, it was in the third week of September. He hadn't held a job for a couple of years, having been fired from his last job on suspicion of severe mental health issues. Something wasn't right with him. Even his wife didn't know."

Sam nodded at Gallagher and said, "You're right. It wasn't just financial. The financial part must be what pushed him over the edge but if you ask me, he was always teetering on that edge. To be honest, don't you think I wish he'd done this back at IIT? That way, he would have been just another unknown joining the many who took the annual pilgrimage by hanging themselves instead of delaying the inevitable and taking five other lives with him. Believe me, I'm just as sickened by this as you. It's hard to keep this all under control. Just thinking of the kids ... I mean who does this to their own kids? Innocent lives, just gone."

"Quite frankly, as disturbed as JV was, he's the one who helped me get through the four years of torture in college. In spite of that, I wish he'd taken his own life back then instead of now.

"This has affected so many lives that it makes me sick. You already know I'm not a family man, and I'm not married, which is by choice. I always thought that JV was not suited for marriage either. Frankly, I don't know why he did get married. I suspect it was family pressure or tradition or societal pressure but it really surprised me to learn that he was married and had kids. In our youth, he had always expressed to me the burden of living with himself. Why would he then burden others if he already knew the kind of burden he was to himself?"

Gallagher reached inside his jacket and pulled out a photograph.

Sam stared at the two young men in that photo staring back at him.

It was an old photo of him and JV outside the US Consulate in Madras in 1985, the day the two of them had gone to apply for their student visas to the United States.

There were no smiles in the photo and Sam had forgotten that it had been taken. But wasn't there a freelance street photographer outside the US Consulate, one who took photos of anyone interested, for a small fee? He recalled that much, but whether that was what they'd done on this day, he couldn't remember despite trying to cast his mind back.

Sam couldn't remember the reason for having the photo taken.

Was it to record a challenging moment in their lives? Or because he knew his time with JV was coming to an end, with graduation around the corner? Gallagher mentioned the detectives said that Sam could keep the photo.

Sam looked at it for a moment and shook his head, passing it back. He didn't know those two young men and quite frankly, he didn't care about them now. Gallagher put it back in his jacket pocket.

Sam thought that JV must have had demons from way back when. Like he had said earlier, maybe the financial situation had been just the tipping point, the final curtain as it were.

All the ingredients were already present, just waiting for the fuse to be lit.

Gallagher had his eyes on Sam as if waiting for him to say something profound and useful to end the meeting with. But Sam didn't have anything else to say, nor even anything else to think about on this ugly matter. This story was over; he had vowed to close this chapter here.

It was better to leave it with that photograph in Gallagher's jacket, an image that belonged nowhere, just like the two people in it. They did not belong anywhere.

As Gallagher stood up as if to end the visit, he handed Sam the manila envelope he had kept under his hands all this time. It had Sam's name on it with a beautiful handwritten print. Even after all these years, Sam recognized JV's handwriting, crisp and clean as always. "For me?" he asked simply completely confused as he stood up to go.

"Yes, for you from JV. I would imagine a parting gift. Now it makes sense that he kept only your number on his phone knowing full well that you would be contacted by the police," said Gallagher. "I am so sorry about this entire thing, Sam. I wish we had met under better circumstances. But in my profession, I tend to meet people in the worst circumstances in their lives. Anyway, the detectives said the case is now closed. You can fly back to New York anytime you wish. Send my best to Jane."

Sam took the folder and walked out thanking Gallagher for all his assistance.

Chapter Nine:

Bygones

Later that evening, Sam realized it had been over twenty years since he'd thought of Amitabh. He looked outside the suite window at the setting sun and thought, "Thank you, Amitabh. In the end, at the very least, you saved me." He recalled that hilarious impression of a drunk Amitabh that JV had put on in his room in front of the mirror. After all these years, Sam could still smile thinking about it. Now, he particularly recalled the last line in which JV said, imitating Amitabh, 'You also go, and I will also go.' Now, he was gone.

Between Sam and JV, one of them had made it out alive and seemed sane, at least for now.

Or am I really mentally sane? Sam wondered. *Perhaps I just have not reached my tipping point. None of us knows what our tipping point is, and mine may come tomorrow, or the next day.*

As adamant as Sam was that he had no tipping point right now, he was also aware that he could not know it either because quite simply, nothing had come along to push him to it.

It seemed probable that his coping skills were more advanced than JV's, and it was likely that his tipping point would never ever be reached, but that didn't mean that there wasn't one.

The following day when he was having his morning coffee, Sam noticed the manila envelope from Gallagher still resting atop the table. He had deliberately not wanted to look inside until now. He was ready now. Opening it, he noticed what looked like a poem and a few sketches. The poem, in English, was written in very nice handwriting by JV's eldest son, Neal.

He had translated it from Hindi, crediting the original author who turned out to be Harivansh Rai Bachchan, none other than Amitabh's father! Things had come full circle somehow. Neal had been following in his father's footsteps.

BYGONES

By Harivansh Rai Bachchan
(Translated by Neal Vishy.)

Let bygones be bygones!
So many people say that this happened with us, that happened with us.
I don't know how we will manage.
My father wrote
'Let bygones be bygones!'
In your life, there was a star.
It's ok if it was close to your heart.
What if it has faded?
Look at the face of the sky;
many of its stars have fallen away,
many of its loved ones went away.
But when does the sky grieve over the fallen stars?

Let bygones be bygones!
In your life, there once was a flower,
over it, you had your life to shower.
What if it has dried and died?
Look at the heart of the garden;
many buds have dried and died,
many saplings have withered away.
Those that dried never bloomed again.
But when does the garden shriek over the dried flowers?
Let bygones be bygones!

Sam pulled out the rest of the papers from the envelope and out came a few incredible sketches of Amitabh Bachchan, all drawn by Neal Vishy. All of the sketches were now of an older Amitabh. He looked the same as Sam remembered him from decades ago, only older. He went through each of the sketches from JV's son, taking his time, marveling at the young man's skill.

Neal Vishy

Neal Vishy

Neal Vishy

Neal Vishy

Along with the sketches were newspaper clippings of articles about Amitabh Bachchan. Sam spent a few moments appreciating the art. JV's eldest son had been incredibly talented. What would the finished product have been if Neal Vishy had been allowed to live and had grown up to be a man?

It had all ended now, and he had to let bygones be bygones just like the poem had said.

Then he slowly opened up the news articles about Amitabh that Neal had clipped, finding a sense of shock at what he learned. Amitabh had been at the height of his fame and fortune in the 1980s, and the last time Sam had seen him in movies or heard about him was from JV in 1985.

Once Sam had moved to the United States, he had forgotten all about Amitabh, like most things in his past. These articles painted a picture that illustrated even the mighty Amitabh was human and susceptible to ego. It seemed likely from reading these pieces that fame and fortune would have some way of letting ego take control, when in fact, a little bit of humility was required.

In a series of unfortunate happenings, both self-inflicted and also hit by outsides forces, Amitabh's fall from the lofty heights had been slow and steady. In a matter of just a few years, Amitabh himself had fallen hard. By the time he reached his fifty-sixth birthday in 1999, Amitabh had been facing bankruptcy, his house in danger of being repossessed.

The government raided his house on suspicion of financial mishandling and incomplete financial disclosures and as a result, he had no bank account left. He had lost everything.

At the age when he should have been secure with a successful and a lifelong career in movies behind him, the great Amitabh had found himself made penniless, with nowhere to go.

He was wallowing in despair, drowning in it.

And it was now, while he was at his lowest moment of despair, that he was offered a lot of money by one of the biggest businessmen in Bombay, an admirer of Amitabh's work.

Despite his desperation, Amitabh refused to take this businessman's gift, not wanting to feel beholden to anyone. No doubt his own ego and a sense of pride won out here too.

Anyone else would probably have jumped at the helping hand and taken the gift but Amitabh seemed to have regained his backbone and his sense of self and that was the turning point.

Rather than take the offered gift, he walked over to one of his neighbors in the affluent neighborhood where the great and good of Bollywood lived. Standing at the door of one the most successful filmmakers in Bollywood, Amitabh begged for a job, any job.

The filmmaker offered Amitabh the role of a father in a new movie he was making.

That role resurrected Amitabh's career and over the next several years, he was cast in hit movie after hit movie and slowly, over much time, he paid back all of his creditors.

Simultaneously, he began to host the Indian version of the television show, 'Who Wants to Be a Millionaire?' Soon, Amitabh was introduced to a new generation of moviegoers.

The rest is history, Amitabh rising like a phoenix back from the ashes.

Sam appreciated the path that Amitabh had taken, recognizing that it was so hard to get to the top of any field. And if you were to tumble from that peak all the way down, then to climb back up again to the top was almost impossible. Yet Amitabh had managed to do that. A rare feat.

And it had taken humility on his part to start the climb back.

Without any doubt, ego was a terrible human trait, perhaps one of the most destructive, being the direct cause of an untold number of failures.

Even the great Amitabh had to be beaten down by fate and self-inflicted wounds before he embraced humility and set aside his ego, to embark on his journey back up to the top.

What irony that Neal Vishy, JV's son, had kept all these articles demonstrating the route back from the brink of disaster. How sad that after leaving his beloved India, JV had never seemed to look to Amitabh for inspiration, for confidence, for humility and to consider his own redemption. The one source of solace upon which JV relied during his four years with Sam, he had seemingly abandoned as soon as they had parted. And just as JV had abandoned Amitabh in his life, a sense of balance, a sense of magic seemed to have vanished from JV's life.

When he needed inspiration in a desperate time, JV didn't have what he'd possessed as a young man. He had no Amitabh to save him. If only he had followed Amitabh as passionately as he had back then, maybe, just maybe, there may have been a different ending to this story.

As Sam picked up the drawings again, admiring the skill, a small, yellowed and dog-eared sheet of folded paper fell to the floor. It looked to have been stuck to the back of the last drawing.

Sam bent down, picked it up and unfolded it with immense care not to tear the thin sheet.

Instantly recognizing JV's handwriting, he tried to flatten it with his palm.

There, written in JV's own inimitably neat hand, was an old translation of a poem by Amitabh Bachchan's father titled, 'Friendship.'

Sam knew the poem and started reading the translation, not because of the poem but because he wanted to see and to immerse himself in JV's handwriting once again. Just for a moment willing to step back into hell, just for a momentary feeling of solace long lost.

It looked as if he had written this right after they'd received their student visas to the United States back in June, 1985. So many years had passed since that time, yet Sam still remembered that beautiful crisp handwriting and could have picked it out in a sea of handwritten notes.

Some verses were illegible, not due to the writing, but perhaps washed away by too much spilled coffee or a few tears. But Sam couldn't help but read it, with a little dampness in his own eyes.

Friendship
A Poem by Harivansh Rai Bachchan.
(Translated by JV, June 1985.)

If I open the story of my memories, some friends come to my mind a lot.
When I think of moments of my past, some friends come to my mind a lot.

Who knows in which town they reside now; they have been away a long time.

When I wake up late at night, some friends come to my mind a lot. Everyone's life has now changed, and life has flowed in a new direction.

No one has time anymore due to work; no one has the need for friends anymore.

Some are busy with learning, some are busy with two lovers. All friends have vanished, those I called 'you' have become 'they.'

When I think of moments of my past, some friends come to my mind a lot.

Slowly, steadily, life gets cut short, life becomes a book of memories.

At times, someone's memory tortures a lot, at times life passes with memories' aid.

Treasures of an ocean don't wash ashore; in life, old friends never return.

Live these moments with a smile, my friend; the season of friendship will never come back.

Sam poured himself a stiff drink, really needing it after the last three days.

The day after that, he went for a drive in and around Los Angeles, just as he'd intended before the detectives had arrived at his hotel suite and crudely pulled him into the past. There were some very good neighborhoods, just like in any other city. He drove by some houses that seemed nice, seemed affordable and seemed to be in good neighborhoods but he was not easily sold on the book based on the cover. At the end of his stay in Los Angeles, Sam spent about five seconds looking at the famed HOLLYWOOD sign, finding that it also did not hold the slightest appeal for him. He didn't see anything special about the iconic sign now.

Dreamers were falling for the make-believe, everything in California seeming out of place. He went back to his home in New York because of it, California unable to hold its charm anymore.

New York, too, seemed empty of its own charm.

But then, wasn't it true that Sam had always been a misfit? So too was JV, neither of them finding a home anywhere. That was the one thing that had drawn this odd pair to each other, and this would have been the answer to Gallagher's impertinent question about what made them friends, if Sam had wanted to try and respond to it. They, he and JV, had not belonged anywhere. And now, JV was gone, passed on to who knew where, to the next life, the next plane in which he maybe also would be out of place.

Sam realized something, which was that unlike JV, he'd never really had that need to belong. This was fortunate for him, and maybe that had been his salvation. This was perhaps why Sam was here to tell the tales of his past, and JV was not here, having ended his past and his present.

The need to belong compromised one's true self in ways that a person did not really notice or understand. He recalled his interview with John Woods of the US Consulate in Madras all those years ago. Sam had been truthful to John Woods back then and had been true to himself ever since, and that had served as his saving grace. He only wished he had been able to make JV be truthful to himself. Then he would have looked at himself with his own eyes instead of the eyes of others, seeing that his situation was never so bad that such an extreme step needed to be taken.

Life was never that bad, and also never that good. You could not make it one way or another.

Life just was, and you had to accept it and get on with it.

Truth would be found lying somewhere in the middle, most of the time. Sam couldn't make JV understand this when he'd had the chance to decades ago, when they were still impressionable.

Sam waited patiently for the next heavy downpour, wanting to wash it all away in nature's blessing. It would surely come sooner or later.

Epilogue

Ronan Doyle

On the day on which he finished writing up Sam Nathan's entire story, Ronan Doyle messaged Sam who requested him to meet him that evening at the same Tapas place as their last meeting.

Ronan walked in with the manuscript in his hand.

Mr. Nathan stood up, shaking Ronan's hand with a warm smile. The last time Ronan had set eyes on him, he had seemed far away despite his politeness. Today, he was warmth itself.

At Mr. Nathan's urging, Ronan ordered mixed platters and red wine for them both and handed over the manuscript to Mr. Nathan, who immediately became lost in its pages. Occasionally, he would look up and smile broadly at Ronan, saying not a word but taking a bite of the snacks or a sip of wine, then falling back into reading. The place was noticeably quiet again, but time seemed to go by quickly.

Mr. Nathan finished reading the manuscript. Then he removed his steel-rimmed glasses and placed them on the table. His eyes smiled and Ronan felt a sense of pride.

My writing did this; it brought a smile to sad eyes, he thought.

Mr. Nathan handed back the manuscript.

"Thank you for bringing my story to life," he said. "This is wonderful work, and you deserve to do what you wish with that manuscript. My only request is that you change the names of all the characters. You were right, you have a gift. You are a pretty good writer."

"Thank you, Mr. Nathan. Coming from you, it means a lot since this was your story."

Mr. Nathan smiled, nodded, and said, "For me, all of this is in the past. A closed book. The entire exercise of writing the story was to help me get past it. Time has helped as well. That script is wonderful, and it sets me free now. As the detectives in Los Angeles said, it is a closed case. I have moved on and wish you all the best. I have a feeling you will do just fine."

Then San Nathan paid the check and stood up.

Ronan stood at the same time, and they shook hands.

As he left, Mr. Nathan said, "You know, if I were looking to hire a writer, I would hire you in a heartbeat."

Ronan replied, "Thank you, Mr. Nathan. I appreciate your belief in me, and the opportunity you gave me."

Mr. Nathan smiled and said that Columbia grads should always look to assist each other, and that down the line, Ronan would have an opportunity to assist another Columbia grad.

Then he stepped out of the Tapas place, the door closing behind him.

The confidence Mr. Nathan instilled in Ronan propelled him to pursue writing on his own, without having to look at being hired by someone else.

He never saw Mr. Nathan ever again, but somehow, Ronan got the feeling that Amitabh had rescued him too. Six degrees of separation from Amitabh Bachchan, perhaps.

In Images:

The Dramatic Fall
of AIG Stock

Chapter Eight tells the catastrophic tale of investor JV's ailing AIG stocks, the catalyst for his downfall. These images may help to put the events into perspective:

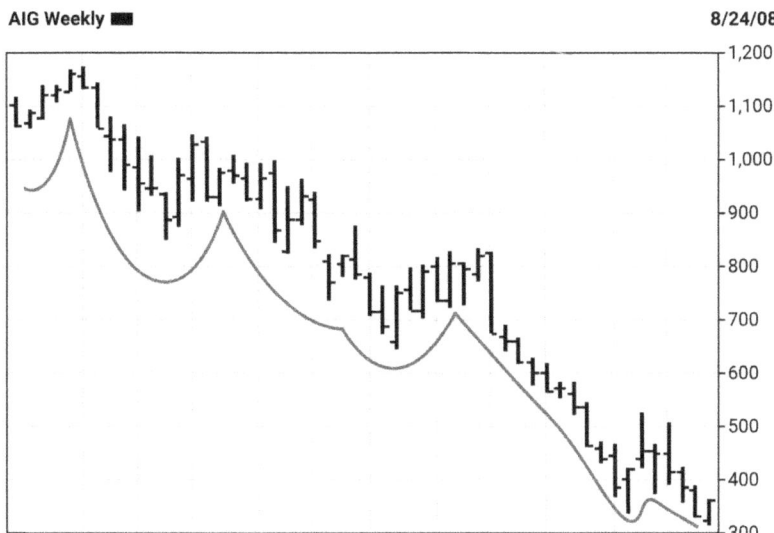

AIG - One year price chart from mid-2007 to August 2008 as the price dropped from over $1200 to below $400

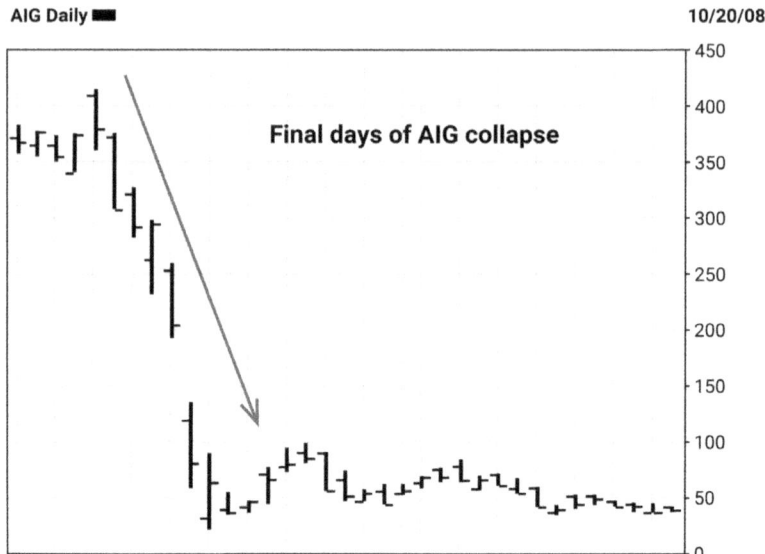

AIG daily price chart in the last days of its collapse in September-October 2008 as AIG falls from over $400 to below $40 in just a matter of days.

www.ingramcontent.com/pod-product-compliance
Lightning Source LLC
Chambersburg PA
CBHW042144170626
46815CB00006BA/306